THE
HARPERS'
HOLIDAY HORROR

A BBLS STORY

By
Elena Southworth

Elena Southworth
www.ElenaSouthworth.com

Cover design and book interior: TheBookMakers.com
Cover illustration: David Harrington

The Harpers' Holiday Horror / Elena Southworth — First Edition
Print ISBN: 978-1-7357829-2-8
eBook ISBN: 978-1-7357829-3-5

Library of Congress Control Number: 2021916150

For Love, Blue, and of course… my LB.
(You know who you are)

Disclaimer:
Mike and Tammy Harper are purely
fictional characters, and NOT based on
my own mom and dad!
(My parents made me add this)

TABLE OF CONTENTS

1

Mission is On

MATTHEW

Sometimes I sit back and wonder what the world would be like without siblings. Younger ones, in my case. If everyone was an only child. I feel it would be fairer, more peaceful, and overall better. Whenever my little sister, Aaliyah, asks for a new toy, Mom will go and buy one for her. Whereas, when I was her age, Mom would make me wait until my birthday if I asked for a toy. If you have a little brother or sister, too, I'm sure you know what I mean. They get everything, they're bossy, they think the world revolves around them, and parents always assume they're innocent.

If they walked out the door and committed a crime, the older sibling would get blamed. If my little sis, Aaliyah, committed a crime, I would be identified as the criminal. Even if I had no clue any of it had happened! Her entire life mission is to be the most irritating little sister on the face of the Earth.

The thing is, Aaliyah always seems to make my mom believe that she's an adorable, auburn-haired, crystal-eyed angel who could never hurt a fly, when really, she's a real piece of work! One of these days, I'm going to walk outside and see a sign taped to a light post with a picture of Aaliyah's face on it saying, "Wanted Dead or Alive!" I think my dad could see right through her, though. He knows her games, but he just doesn't seem to care. So instead, he lets Aaliyah do what she wants.

Adults take one look at that girl, and suddenly, Aaliyah Jasmine Harper is not a high-maintenance, naughty little kid. Adults take one look at *any* little kid, and the bad thing they did was no longer their fault. My mom calls Aaliyah "The Baby." She's almost nine-years-old! I'm being serious here! Aaliyah is always doing something that isn't allowed, but my mom still thinks she's blameless. If I, on the other hand, did just one bad thing, I'd be grounded! You see what I mean? Probably not yet, but walk a mile in my old, muddy, beaten-up sneakers, and you will. You will understand me, even if I'm the criminal.

Aaliyah

I've had this theory since I was about four years old called The Matthew Making Theory. That my eighteen-year-old brother Matthew is an alien from a high-tech spaceship full of other aliens. So these aliens have babies that aren't born babies, but teenagers! Then the aliens would disguise the teenage babies as *human* teenagers and send them down to Earth to pick on kids like me. It all made sense! According to my research—I like to think of myself as a scientist, by the way—in the alien world, human data is uploaded into the teenagers' brains so that they know how to act human on Earth. Maybe schools that teenagers go to here on Earth consist of top-secret alien experiments. The staff members and teachers are actually scientists trying to find out the truth. Or maybe they are aliens, too!

This has gotten to the point where I have to know the truth. I've been thinking about all of this for half my life. I'm worried that one of these days, I might be taken over by aliens. Or, what if I already was one?!

I haven't seen Matthew since he left to go to college in late August. Now it is November and he is coming home for the holidays! So here's what I am going to do: I will start a mission to find out the truth about Matthew. I'll spy on him! Maybe when teenagers spend all twenty-four hours of the day behind their closed bedroom door, only coming out to eat, they are meeting with their fellow aliens! I've grown up around teenagers my whole life. I don't have any memories of Matthew before he was a teenager. I also have an older sister, Camille, who was thirteen when I was born. And I must say, TEENAGERS NEVER LEAVE THEIR ROOMS! The only reasonable explanation is because they are aliens! They *must* be! I need to know! Mission is on.

MATTHEW

I was glad to be going back home in a few days, until I got a call from Mom and Dad and found out some really bad news. To celebrate Thanksgiving break and Aaliyah's ninth birthday, which is on December 1st, we will be taking a one-week vacation to the Grand Canyon. You know what happens on a vacation that involves Aaliyah? She does something crazy, and the entire trip gets ruined. When we went to Hawaii for my high school graduation and eighteenth birthday in August—actually, let's not bring that up. The gist is, things did not go well. We came home in bad condition: I had a tan line on my back that spelled out "Punch Me," Aaliyah had sun poisoning, and Dad and our oldest sister, Camille pretended they were part of another family. Mom was still as loud and obnoxious as she always was.

BBLS, which stands for Big Brother Little Sister, is a code word that me and Aaliyah came up with a few years ago. We use it whenever we go on a big adventure together. I try to tell Aaliyah not to get us into BBLS trouble when we are out, but it never seems to help. She always ruins our outings. Chances are this trip would be no different.

Aaliyah

Early in the evening, I was sitting in my room playing with my toys and trying to pass the time. Matthew was coming home from college today, and I was very excited to start my mission. I was getting impatient. I couldn't wait for him to arrive! Then, all of a sudden, I heard the doorbell ring. I looked out my window and checked the cars out front. There was a big gray car, a pizza delivery car, and then... Matthew's dented car! A wave of eagerness and suspense rushed over me. It was time! I crept downstairs to the front door like a spy on the lookout for a criminal or a mad scientist about to make a breakthrough discovery.

I was the only one who seemed to care about Matthew's homecoming, though. Mom was upstairs in her room giving herself a facial, and Dad was on the couch watching sports and waiting for a pizza delivery. I bet my entire life savings that if it were me who had returned home, the door would have been knocked down by Mom's excitement. I am the Golden Child, by the way. Being Mom's favorite is great and all, but I have to admit that sometimes I feel sorry for my siblings. I don't know why I'm the favorite. Mom always said it's because Matthew and Camille are older than me, and they don't need her as much anymore, but I still don't know.

I yanked the door open, screaming hello as I gave Matthew a playful shove.

Only... it wasn't Matthew. It was a grumpy guy delivering Dad's pizza! I thought I would faint from embarrassment. He gave me a confused look.

"Pizza delivery for Mike Harper?"

"Yup, that's my daddy," I said.

Dad yelled at me from the living room. "Aaliyah! Bring me my pizza! Give him the money on the counter."

I took the box of pizza from the guy's hands, gave him the money, and slammed the door. I was mad and *so* embarrassed! Where was Matthew? I saw his car out there! I really thought it would be him at the door. I gave Dad his pizza. Then I walked out the front door and went over to Matthew's car, and there he was, in the front seat on his phone. I banged on the window.

"Hey Aaliyah!" He looked up from his phone and yelled through the glass.

"That's my name!" I smiled. Finally! I could begin my mission.

MATTHEW

"Mom? Dad? I'm home!" Neither of them came to say hello. When are they ever going to notice me? Aaliyah looked different. Her hair was longer, and it seemed like she was trying to grow out her bangs. I went upstairs and banged on the bathroom door. I could hear opera music playing and Mom's shrill voice singing. Ack. Probably not a great idea to knock again. She loses her mind when people interrupt her during her facials. I headed back downstairs and said hi to Dad. He seemed more interested in his basketball game than in me.

Aaliyah and I went up to my room. She told me that she had mistaken the pizza delivery guy for me. So we wrote about it in our secret journal, for all our adventures and inside jokes. One day we will look back at it and laugh.

About an hour later, Mom came out of the bathroom and finally said hello. Then she ran over to "The Baby's" room to start packing for the big trip. Mom seriously favors Aaliyah. I don't know what it is about that naughty third-grade sister of mine that Mom treasures so much! Of course, mom couldn't care less about Camille, our oldest sister, either. *Sigh.* It's always the youngest one that people seem to like the most. I don't know why.

Aaliyah and I walked into her room to find Mom filling up a lacey pink suitcase to the brim with clothes. Once again, Aaliyah gets something new. That suitcase. Even though she got one when we left for our vacation to Hawaii a few months ago. *My* suitcase is twelve years old! I ask Mom for a new one each time we travel, but the answer is always the same: "No, the one you have is high quality and perfectly functional." That's the answer, even though I am in desperate need of a new one. Are you asking why? Oh, I'll tell you why. My suitcase is cracking in nearly twenty different areas. There is duct tape on one of the corners. Also, it's covered in colorful smiling dinosaurs. My suitcase looks like it belongs to a four-year-old who tied it to a tricycle with a jump rope and rode it around a playground.

Aaliyah is going to be *trouble* in the future if Mom and Dad kept up with their parenting choices. I mean, she kinda already is. Sometimes I look at her and think, *this kid's gonna be the reason I go to jail*. I can't even tell you how many times we've had to call 911 on her. Once it was because she got us stuck in a tube slide. When we were in Hawaii, she was on a first-name basis with the fire department. That "vacation" was really just the biggest mess. Aaliyah and Mom drove the rest of us crazy. Even Camille, who loves kids and is now working on her teaching credential, couldn't wait to get away from Aaliyah. I have actual panic attacks just thinking of the future and what it holds.

Anyway, let's get back to the story.

2

Gangster Grannies

Aaliyah

Things just kept on getting worse since Matthew got home. That night, my twenty-one-year-old sister Camille—or Cami—as Matthew and I call her—also came home from school. She, for some reason; is trying to become a teacher. Now this is something I just don't understand. Why would she choose to be a teacher when she could be a movie stunt person, race car driver, or astronaut?! Now, that would be cool!

The five of us sat down on the couch for a talk. Mom was enthusiastic about her "good" news. Poor Dad sat there with a sour face, waiting to un-pause the TV.

"Children, we have a special holiday treat for you!" Mom squealed. "Your Grandma Pearl and Grandma Agnes are going to join us for the holidays!" We exchanged worrisome looks, waiting for someone to speak.

MATTHEW

Uh-oh. This can't be good. Before you come at me for not being excited about seeing my grandmas, let me explain.

It all started maybe ten years ago, before Aaliyah was even born, when both our grandpas passed away, months apart. Ever since then, Grandma Pearl and Grandma Agnes sort of just... ganged up. They became best friends. Grandma Pearl started visiting Grandma Agnes at her house every single day to ride their motorcycles around the street at top speed, listen to heavy metal music in the garage at full volume, and yell at any neighbors who confronted them. Finally, the next-door neighbors got so fed up that they packed their things and moved away. And then... Grandma Pearl bought their house! So now they live right next to each other! It's gotta be the loudest, most chaotic neighborhood in the universe. Who would've ever thought that seventy-eight-year-old grandmas were like that? Every time they've visited, terrible things happened. Not once, not twice, but repeatedly until they finally left. We couldn't wait to get them out of the house! That's where

Aaliyah gets her naughty traits from. It's like mischief runs in the family. It didn't always used to be like this, though. My grandmas were once rivals. They would fight over things that literally had no significance, like whose eyelashes were longer. I don't know what changed.

This news can't be good at all.

Camille

Alright, let me get this straight. My little sister is about to turn nine (even though she has the behavior skills of a two-year-old), my mom still doesn't know how to raise a kid after twenty-one years of experience, and most importantly, Grandma Pearl and Grandma Agnes are coming to celebrate with us?

Right now I have no words.

MATTHEW

We three siblings sat down in my room. We needed some time to discuss the current situation.

"Aaliyah, you are usually a problem, but at least there's only one of you. Now, with the Grandmas coming, that means three big problems!" I told her.

"I promise I won't be much trouble," she replied. "Because trust me, I know what we're about to go through."

Aaliyah

Things got worse the day before Thanksgiving. Mom left for the store in the morning and she was gone for quite some time. I got worried. I could only imagine what she was up to.

Anyways, remember what I said about The Matthew Making Theory? Well, now is my chance to start spying on Matthew to see what he is always doing in his room and if it's true that he talks to aliens. Dad has a camcorder that he's used for past vacations, so I asked if I could borrow it. As usual, he was too wrapped up in his TV show to listen, so he nodded his head and mumbled. I took it as a yes. I got the camcorder from the closet and set it up in Matthew's room while he was downstairs getting food. I couldn't wait to see!

When Mom came back home, she was carrying dozens of bags. That wasn't the bad part, though. It got much more intense. A big delivery truck pulled into our driveway. Mom opened the garage. A few workers got out of the truck and lined up one by one, with Mom yelling as she directed them. Startled, Dad bolted up from the couch and ran to the door.

"Whoa, whoa, whoa! Tammy, what is going on?" he asked Mom. The workers removed a mattress from the truck and started hauling it inside. Mom directed the workers as they carried it into our house.

"That's it, you guys! Steady, steady! Keep a good pace! I believe in all of you!" It turns out, Mom had bought two twin size beds. One for each grandma. The men continued to haul the furniture out of the truck. Dad turned to Mom.

"Tammy! What is happening?!"

"I bought our moms a bedroom set for their stay!" She screamed—I mean said—joyfully.

"A bedroom set?" He watched the workers move our living room furniture into the garage to make room for the beds.

"Yeah, what's the problem?" Mom replied.

"Tammy! We're staying in a hotel near the Grand Canyon, remember? They are only spending one night here, and we were planning on having them sleep on mattresses on the floor! You didn't need to get actual furniture!"

"Mike, I—I just thought it would make their experience with us more luxurious!" Mom yipped. She just wasn't getting it.

"Tammy! We don't need any of this! Let's return all of it." Dad walked over to the driver and told him to take the beds back to the store.

"Sorry sir, our store is shutting down. All sales are final. We're not taking returns," said the driver. Dad sighed.

I picked up one of the bags and looked inside. *What did she get?* It contained high-quality shampoo, lotion, and other self-care products. Probably for herself. I picked up the biggest bag. It was filled with toys. Yay! They must be for me. I opened more bags. They were all filled with more toys! Then I felt guilty. What if those were for my birthday?

Or Christmas? Oh, well. Mom wasn't gonna care if I saw them.

MATTHEW

Our entire living room was ripped out. In place of the couch and coffee table were two beds, one for Grandma Pearl and the other for Grandma Agnes.

As it turned out, the beds weren't the only things Mom purchased. The delivery workers also brought in a dresser, a desk, a nightstand, lamps, piles of bedding, and even photo frames. You name it, Mom bought it.

When Dad saw the workers hanging up curtains on the windows in the living room, he stomped upstairs to his and Mom's room and slammed the door.

"I hope you all realize that we are selling all of this since we can't return it!" he shouted.

I decided to call my girlfriend Delaney Emerson, who would be coming over tomorrow night with her family for Thanksgiving dinner and traveling with us to the Grand Canyon. I am really anxious about this trip. Not only would we have feisty Aaliyah, but also Delaney's parents, her frustrating little sister, Mindy, who turned ten last month, AND Mom AND the grandmas.

When I went to my room to call Delaney, I noticed Dad's camcorder sitting on my dresser. A red light was flashing from it. What—WAIT. I was being videotaped! What is Aaliyah up to now? It was definitely Aaliyah who set that up! If she really wanted to film me, she should have at least hidden the camcorder, not left it in the middle of my dresser with the red record light flashing. Common sense, people! Common sense!

Delaney

I've known Matthew Harper for about eleven years now. We had gone to the same elementary school, middle school, and high school, went to prom together, and ended up getting into the same university. Our dorms are even in walking distance to each other. Basically, we are like childhood sweethearts. We both have little sisters, Mindy and Aaliyah, so we have the same adventures—and problems.

I know quite a bit about Matthew's grandmas. In elementary school, whenever the teacher would ask about what we did over holiday breaks, Matthew would raise his hand and say something about how his grandmas came to visit and blew up their kitchen trying to cook. Or how they dropped an extra-large double-patty bacon cheeseburger into the public pool, or something else equally wild.

One time, in the beginning of fourth grade, our class was writing an essay about our summer vacation. When everyone was finished, we got to present them to the class. Matthew wrote about how his grandmas, Pearl and Agnes, came to visit and left the water in the upstairs bathtub running all night. They closed all the doors so nobody would hear it and put the plug in the drain, so the entire bathroom flooded. Water seeped underneath the flooring and into the walls and caused a mold issue. Their family had to stay in a hotel for the rest of the summer while a repair crew came to dry it all out and put in new floors. I think that happened a few months before Aaliyah was born, so if they could cause all that trouble *without* Aaliyah, I couldn't imagine what would happen *with* her around. Or with Mindy being with them as well. She is surprisingly not too bad when she's by herself, but throw her with someone like Aaliyah, and she gets BAD. Aaliyah is always talking Mindy into doing something ridiculous.

Tomorrow is Thanksgiving, and me, Mom, Dad, and Mindy will spend it at Matthew's house. Mindy and Aaliyah are best friends, so Aaliyah has invited us to travel with them for her birthday. We would leave together the next day.

I am petrified about this trip. We are going to have Mindy, Aaliyah, Grandma Pearl, *and* Grandma Agnes. Four trouble-seekers. Five, if you count Mrs. Harper, Matthew's mom. She's the reason Aaliyah is such a nightmare. So, yeah. Five trouble-seekers.

3

A Rude Awakening

Tammy Harper

I can't believe that Queen Baby Aaliyah will be NINE in a couple of days! She's getting so old and is still so young. She's just such a little princess! I love taking The Baby on shopping sprees. I buy her whatever she wants! I should take her to the new toy store that just opened... I'd love to post pictures of it!

Aaliyah

Well, I guess Matthew found the camcorder. It's okay, though. I'll try again, but right now I have something way more important on my mind. We all do. Grandma Pearl and Grandma Agnes will be here soon for Thanksgiving dinner.

Camille

I heard the doorbell ring and braced myself. *Here comes trouble.*

It turned out to be Mr. and Mrs. Emerson, Delaney, and Mindy. I relaxed a bit. My siblings, along with Delaney and Mindy, discussed different coping methods for dealing with the grandmas.

My relief didn't last long because Grandma Pearl and Grandma Agnes eventually made their debut.

"Children!" Mom roared. *Why is she so loud?* "Your grandmas are here!"

Alright, Cami, I told myself. *Just go and say hi.* Well, here goes nothing...

Aaliyah

Our group went downstairs to see Grandma Pearl and Grandma Agnes standing at the door. Grandma Agnes had a walker, and Grandma Pearl had a cane. All of a sudden, I felt very relieved. If they needed equipment to help them walk, then maybe they couldn't get into so much trouble! Boy was I wrong...

There was a cute, fluffy little puppy on a thin leash next to them. Aww, adorable!

The sound of screams pierced my ears. You see, when Matthew was younger, he was bitten by a big stray dog. He's been terrified of dogs ever since.

"AAAAAAAAAAAAAAAA!!!!!!!!!!!!!! GET THAT WOLF AWAY FROM ME!" Matthew hollered and went running up the stairs. I understand why he'd be afraid, but really. This thing was just a cotton ball, no bigger than a bunny. What a baby.

Delaney

A few months ago, Aaliyah broke her ankle at school. When Matthew and I went to visit her in the hospital, an older man started walking out with his dog. Embarrassed, I ended up having to give Matthew a piggyback ride into the hospital because he was so scared of the dog. Why haven't I dumped that dork yet?

"What's your puppy's name?" I asked Grandma Agnes.

"Chicken," she replied.

I looked at her and laughed. "No, really, what's his name?" I asked again.

"I just told you, little missy. This is Chicken."

I bent down and looked at his collar. There was a small blue charm in the shape of a bone that read, "Chicken."

Wow. She was actually being serious. What a way to ruin an adorable puppy!

"Come on inside!" Mrs. Harper said in a booming voice. "I made some scrumptious, gooey, warm cookies!" I licked my lips. That sounded good!

It turns out, the cookies were even worse than Chicken's name. They were tasteless, healthy oatmeal cookies and hard as a rock. I saw Mom spit hers out while Mrs. Harper wasn't looking. I watched as she hid it in her pocket for a few minutes, then fed it to Chicken who was under her feet. I don't think she realized I was watching her.

I went up to Matthew's room to find him. I walked in and saw him buried under a fort made with blankets.

"I-i-i-i-i-sss the w-wolf gone?" he stuttered.

"Matthew. That thing's name is literally Chicken."

Chicken

I sniffed around. The loud lady named "Tammy" smelled very overwhelming, like a mix of strong perfume and hair bleach. I choked on the fumes. Some other lady was feeding me bits of a tasteless cookie. Food is food, and I love food! So, I ate it anyway.

4

Thanksgiving Terror

Aaliyah

Mom cooked dinner while Dad was at the store getting last-minute items. Mindy and I went to my room to play with our dolls. We were brushing their hair, and then we thought it would be fun to style *our* hair, too.

I found Mom's hair lightening spray in her room. It is supposed to make your hair blonde just by spraying it. That would be so cool! We wanted to try it on our hair, but I wasn't sure if it would actually work, so I told Mindy we should try it on someone else's hair first. That way, if it didn't work, their hair would be destroyed and not ours.

We asked Matthew, Delaney, Cami, and even the grandmas, but nobody would volunteer. We didn't want to ask Mom because then she would spend the rest of the night annoying us about beauty products. So really the only option left was to try it on the puppy, Chicken.

Mindy put Chicken in my doll makeover chair. She gave him one of Mom's gross cookies, and he sat there happily eating it up. I took a deep breath and sprayed his brown fur with the blonde spray bottle. It smelled disgusting.

It was a good thing we tried it on Chicken, because we learned that we should *never* use that stuff on our own hair.

Mindy

Using the spray on Chicken was an epic failure. His fur was almost... purple? I couldn't even identify it. In just a matter of minutes, Chicken had gone from being the cutest dog I'd ever seen to one of the worst. We were going to be in such big trouble!

Aaliyah got a hair buzzer from the bathroom and said our best choice was to shave his fur off. She took the buzzer and shaved a line down Chicken's back. Only then, we heard footsteps!

"Aaliyah! Mindy! Come down! It's time for our Thanksgiving dinner!" It was Mr. Harper's voice.

OH NO!!!! We grabbed blankets, a towel, and shirts from inside the closet and shoved them on top of Chicken. Anything to hide him!

But we were too late.

MATTHEW

When Dad got home from the store, every terrible thing possible happened. Me, Cami, and Delaney had set the table, and we were getting ready to have our Thanksgiving dinner. Dad went upstairs to get Mindy and Aaliyah. Then, we heard him yelling in anger. Oh no, had something happened? I ran upstairs with Mom and Cami.

When we stepped into Aaliyah's room, there was some purple stuffed animal that I didn't know Aaliyah even had lying in the middle of the floor. Aaliyah and Mindy appeared guilty and looked at us with lopsided smiles. The stuffed animal started moving and licking cookie crumbs off the floor! Then I realized... that was no stuffed animal! It was that wolf Grandma Pearl and Grandma Agnes had brought! The thing was unrecognizable. His fur was a nauseating purple, and he had a hairless line going down his back!

"What did you girls do?!" Dad hollered at Aaliyah and Mindy.

"Mike!" Mom hissed. "Don't yell at The Baby! She's only eight!" She turned to Aaliyah. "Aaliyah-Bubbiya, that hair bleach isn't meant for dogs, but if your dream is to be a hairstylist, then pursue your dreams, sugar-pie! Pursue your dreams! You'll improve! Oh, Mike, she's just so passionate! The Baby has the brightest future!" Aaliyah giggled nervously. Mindy, standing guiltily in the corner, explained that they had been going to try it on themselves.

"Well, sweetie pie, if you and Queen Aaliyah wanted to bleach your hair, all you had to do was tell me and I would've taken you to the salon," Mom said in an excited voice.

I wanted to scream! If I had done that, I would've been in so much trouble! Even when I was Aaliyah's age, Mom never would've let me get away with that. How come Aaliyah is different? I hid behind Cami, still scared of the dog. He looked so purple and small. I kinda felt bad for him. "That's it." Dad grunted. He walked over and picked up the purple dog. "I'm really frustrated with you, Aaliyah. You guys are so lucky it is Thanksgiving. Aaliyah, that's the only reason you aren't grounded. Just look at the poor dog! Now, we're going to go down and have a nice, peaceful Thanksgiving dinner with Pearl and my mom. I don't want to hear another word spoken from anybody!"

Little did we know that dinner would be nowhere near "nice and peaceful."

Camille

As if that whole doggy hair salon situation wasn't bad enough, when we got downstairs, Grandma Pearl and Grandma Agnes had gotten into some mischief. Unbelievable. They haven't even been here for an hour!

They had eaten about half of the dinner! Grandma Agnes—who, by the way, was "in a walker"—was STANDING up on the table and dancing! What was going on?! She jumped down, grabbed a turkey leg, and bit a big piece off. We all watched in shock. Why didn't the Emerson's try to stop them? Mr. and Mrs. Emerson had been standing in a corner watching the nightmare unfold with dropped jaws. Both grandmas were cackling hysterically. Grandma Pearl grabbed a candle from the countertop.

"AAH! HOT! HOT! HOT!" She threw it at the table. *Well duh, it's fire. Of course it's hot.* The candle smashed, and the entire table quickly caught fire! The fire alarm in the room started blaring. I grabbed a blanket and threw it on top of the fire, desperately trying to put it out!

"I'm going to call the fire department!" Mr. Emerson shouted to Dad.

"No, don't! I've got it under control," Dad said with desperation in his voice.

Mr. Emerson shrugged. My guess is that Dad didn't want to deal with another 911 situation. We'd already had enough in Hawaii. It's very embarrassing.

Matthew and Dad ran outside and grabbed the hose. Together, they began spraying the burning table. Everything got soaked and the fire alarm stopped. A fire extinguisher would have been a better choice.

When the commotion was over, Mom and Dad stared at our table and what remained of our Thanksgiving dinner. It was completely burned and inedible. I coughed from the smoke. Grandma Pearl and Grandma Agnes were rolling on the floor with laughter.

"BOOM! EXPLOSIVE!" they screamed.

Mom grabbed Aaliyah by the arms and screamed right in her ear. "ARE YOU HURT?!" Of course, Mom only cared about Aaliyah!

"Don't you guys have any respect? You know what? I'm not buying new plates and utensils, and Tammy is not making another dinner! You can either make your own or starve!" Dad yelled and stomped away. "Every single time we try to do something nice," he muttered under his breath as he left the room and made his way upstairs.

Dad never came back down that night. We dug through the fridge, freezer, and pantry for anything that would make a good dinner. We ended up eating stale crackers and frozen microwavable macaroni and cheese that Aaliyah found at the bottom of the freezer drawer. We ate ON THE FLOOR, mind you, since the table was a burned wreck.

The mac and cheese was horrible. It smelled weird and tasted almost like... fish? I ate as little as possible, fearing it would give me food poisoning. I looked at the box. The ingredients seemed normal. But then... I saw the expiration date. No wonder it was so gross! That slimy stuff had expired almost two years ago and had freezer burn!

Grandma Pearl and Grandma Agnes had the worst manners while we ate. They were burping, chewing with their mouths wide open, and mashing up their food then shoving it into their mouths with their hands. I was sitting in between both of them. It was disgusting!

Sitting across from me was Aaliyah, who was being spoon-fed by Mom and making the weirdest faces with each new scoop of food.

"Um, Cami," Matthew whispered to me. I smelled something rancid. Something right in front of me smelled like rotted meat. I looked down and made a horrifying discovery. Grandma Pearl had taken out her dentures and put them on my plate, right in my food! Ugh! Yuck! Mr. and Mrs. Emerson, who hadn't said a word all night, exchanged disgusted looks.

"Mom, put your teeth back in." Mom whispered to Grandma Pearl. Mom was getting completely on my nerves, too. I got angrier with every scoop of food she force-fed Aaliyah.

I heard barking. Chicken, the purple, half-shaved puppy entered the room. Grandma Pearl and Grandma Agnes, instead of being mad at Aaliyah and Mindy, actually THANKED them and said that they liked Chicken's new look! Wow. Just wow.

When we got up, the grandmas ditched their walking equipment completely.

"We only use these to create an image," Grandma Pearl explained. "So whenever we cause a ruckus, people won't suspect that it's the poor ol' ladies." She and Grandma Agnes laughed evilly. Aaliyah rolled her eyes as Mom put another spoonful of that garbage mac-and-cheese in her mouth.

I'm dreading this trip.

5

The Wedding Cake

MATTHEW

That was by far the worst Thanksgiving ever. The food we *did* get to eat was so gross. I didn't even have the slightest clue what it was. I didn't want to be rude, so I picked at it pretending to eat. I saw Delaney, Mindy, Cami, and Mr. and Mrs. Emerson doing the same thing. Poor Aaliyah had no choice since she was being fed by Mom. Just the smell of it made me all queasy. It didn't help that Grandma Pearl and Grandma Agnes had the manners of barnyard animals.

When it was time for the Emersons to leave, they practically ran out the door. Mr. Emerson was going so fast trying to get to his car, he stumbled and belly-flopped right into the bushes.

I went to bed that night hungry and anxious. At midnight, I was still lying wide awake, feeling worried. I really didn't want to go on this trip. In just a few hours, so much had already happened. I couldn't imagine traveling with this whole group of people for a week!

I was so hungry I felt sick, so I got up and tip-toed downstairs to the kitchen to get a snack. Grandma Pearl and Grandma Agnes, who were sleeping on the new beds in the living room, were snoring like pigs. I gagged. I heard noises coming from the coat closet and decided to check it out. I opened the door. I found Dad sitting in there, holding Chicken and watching basketball on his phone. He looked up at me.

"Alright, Matthew," he whispered. "We have five hours to plot an escape."

Mindy

When we left the Harpers' house on Thanksgiving, Mrs. Harper loaded a lifetime supply of presents into our car for Aaliyah's birthday. She didn't want to keep them in their car because Aaliyah would see them. Why were there so many?

On the drive back home my parents talked about how dysfunctional the Harpers were.

"Delaney, why are you still with Matthew?" Dad asked.

"Yeah," Mom agreed. "He's got problems and so does the rest of his nut-job family."

"I dunno, I guess it's just because I've known him my entire life. I mean, he's a good boyfriend, but yeah. I've honestly never been a fan of Aaliyah or his parents. Cami isn't so bad, though," Delaney said.

I looked over at Delaney and she was red with embarrassment.

"Aaliyah is amazing. What are you talking about?" I said, defending my best friend.

The next morning, we got up early to get ready for the trip. Aaliyah and I both agreed to bring our dolls, so I packed mine before we left. I was excited to see Aaliyah, but I really didn't want to see her grandmas. Especially not after last night.

Aaliyah

BBLS. What can I say? It's our game, all about annoying each other. Mom decided to "sing" a "song" on the drive, to help pass the time. At first, I was terrified. Her voice is ear-shattering. But then I realized mine is, too, so it would be fun to bother Matthew, Cami, and Dad! We started singing nursery rhymes. Even Grandma Pearl and Grandma Agnes chimed in! Then Chicken decided to become a part of the fun, howling along to our songs! I looked at Matthew, Cami, and Dad. They all had tears in their eyes. I choked on my own laughter.

Camille

"6,000 BOTTLES OF MILK ON THE WALL, 6,000 BOTTLES OF MILK! TAKE ONE DOWN, PASS IT AROUND, 5,999 BOTTLES OF MILK ON THE WALL! OLD MAC-AALIYAH HAD A FARM!!! E-I-E-I-O!!!!!!!!!!! AND ON THAT FARM SHE HAD A COW!!!! E-I-E-I-O!!!!!!!!"

That's what I had to listen to for the entire three and a half hours we drove. Mom, Aaliyah, and the grandmas were all caterwauling at the top of their lungs, and Chicken was barking nonstop. How were their throats not sore yet?! I saw Dad and Matthew clenching their jaws and fists. The three of us had the biggest headaches of our lives that day.

"Oh, for crying out loud! Can't you guys just be quiet for FIVE minutes?!" Matthew yelled.

"Yeah, you guys, I need it to be quiet in here," Dad said, his hands squeezed tight on the steering wheel. "I can't focus on the road with all the noise. I need to concentrate on driving so I don't get in an accident." Dad groaned. Aaliyah laughed. She is so immature. It seems like every year she's getting worse.

When we finally arrived at the hotel, I nearly collapsed on the ground. My head was pounding. My ears were ringing. My eyes were all watery. There were black spots in my vision. Even Matthew was complaining that his head hurt.

We checked into our room, which was a very nice two-bedroom suite. One room was for our family and the attached bedroom had two twin-sized beds for the grandmas. There was even a small kitchen. The Emersons checked into their room, just down the hall from ours. While Mom, Aaliyah, Chicken, and the grandmas went back to the car to unload our luggage, we three normal people stayed back at the hotel. Our heads hurt too much to help. We all lied in bed, the room dark and the curtains tightly closed. It was misery.

* * *

My headache was a little better that evening. Mom and I went to a nearby bakery to buy Aaliyah a birthday cake. Dad and Mr. and Mrs. Emerson took Aaliyah, Mindy, Matthew, and Delaney to a park to play in the snow.

Inside the bakery, there were rows of pastries and baked goods. I wanted to eat all of it! On one of the shelves was an enormous three-layer cake covered in swirls, white frosting, and pink roses. There was a piece of paper next to it that read, "Ready for purchase. $300." Mom approached the baker.

"Hello, tomorrow is my baby's birthday. I'd like to purchase this pretty cake," she said in a sweet tone, pointing to the big fancy one. I slapped my palm to my forehead. It was way too large and expensive!

"Oh, ma'am, that's actually a wedding cake. Baby cakes are over here." He pointed to another shelf that had cakes frosted in light pink and blue with "Baby's First Birthday" written on top.

"Don't you tell me what to do and how to celebrate my child!" Mom pointed her manicured finger at him. Uh oh, she was offended. "If I say I want this cake, then obviously The Baby deserves it! Like, she's turning nine! It's such an accomplishment!"

The baker stared back at her, his mouth gaping open. I was SO embarrassed! I gave him an apologetic look, mouthed "sorry" and tried to talk some sense into Mom.

"Okay, Mom, don't you think this cake may be a little too big? It's for a wedding, and weddings usually have hundreds of guests. There are only eleven of us."

"The bigger, the better, Camille! The bigger, the better!" she squealed. I gave up. It was no use. Once Mom set's her mind on something, there's no possible way of talking her out of it unless you have superhuman powers.

Mom bought the wedding cake. The baker packed it into a tremendously huge pink box for us.

On the drive back to the hotel, the cake was so big and heavy that it reached from my lap to the roof of the car. Mom put me in charge of making sure it was safe. I even had to wrap my seatbelt around me *and* the box with the cake in it! That thing had to have weighed a thousand pounds. It was so heavy my legs became numb! Then I got in an entire workout trying to carry it into the hotel lobby. We had to ask the hotel manager to store it in their refrigerator. There was no way the nine-year-old's three-hundred-dollar "birthday" cake was going to fit in the tiny fridge in our room. The poor manager looked really annoyed.

After that whole bakery experience, I decided not to mention to Mom that we hadn't gotten any balloons or decorations. If that was Mom's idea of a cake, I didn't even want to know what she'd get for decorations.

6

Birthdays and Babies

Aaliyah

Today, December 1st, is my birthday. I am nine!

I was woken up by Mom's squawking. "HAPPY BIRTHDAY TO THE UNICORN-MERMAID-FAIRY PRINCESS, AALIYAH!"

I cracked my eyes open and checked the time. *6:00 a.m.* No wonder the room was pitch black. What was she thinking?

"Can my dolly come, too?" I asked, taking my small doll out of my suitcase. We were going ice skating with the Emersons.

"OF COURSE!" she yelled, waking up the rest of our family. I winced once more at the noise.

After getting breakfast and meeting up with Mindy and her family, we planned to walk down to the frozen pond across the street where people can rent ice skates. Mom went back to our room to put Chicken in his crate. We waited outside for an eternity. What was Mom doing?! How long does it take to put a small purple puppy in his crate?! I went back to the room to see what was taking her so long and found her in the bathroom doing her makeup while a soap opera played in the background.

"Come on in, sweetie pie! I'm going to give you a makeover!" she screeched.

"But Mom—" A makeover? Seriously? We were only going ice skating! Mom ignored me and gave me a whole makeover. She put on layers of necklaces and a ton of makeup. She even trimmed my bangs, which I had been trying to grow out! I could hear everyone else banging at the door, yelling at us to hurry up. Mom locked them out and wouldn't open the door.

"Angelic baby Aaliyah, this is my designer purse. I want you to put your belongings in it for ice skating," Mom said and handed me an expensive-looking white leather purse with a ribbon and gold chain.

"Wow! Mom, it's pretty, but this isn't a fashion show. You don't have to do this." She refused to take it back. Oh well. I put my doll and water bottle inside. I felt a hint of worry in my stomach. What if something happens to the purse?

Mom finally put Chicken in his little crate in the grandmas' room. She pushed the door closed, but it had some fancy lock and she couldn't figure out how it worked. We decided to leave him out of the crate. I mean, he is a good puppy. What could happen?

Delaney

We got to the frozen pond and already there was a problem. Aaliyah asked to go to the bathroom.

"Of course, sweetie pie!" Mrs. Harper shouted. Aaliyah walked to the bathroom, which was a single outdoor stall. She closed the door and locked it. Matthew needed to go too, so of course Aaliyah started up a BBLS fight. She was taking a long time just to annoy him.

"Aaliyah!" Matthew yelled through the door.

"That's my name!" she responded.

"Hurry up! I'm waiting!" He tried turning the doorknob. It had been a few minutes, and it was about time for Aaliyah to be wrapping things up.

"Wait, but the door is stuck! This lock isn't working! I'm trapped inside!" Aaliyah shouted. Matthew rolled his eyes. She was totally lying. Mindy does this to me, too, sometimes.

It turns out that she wasn't lying. Ten minutes passed as we tried to get the lock unstuck. That thing was absolutely jammed! Mrs. Harper was starting to freak out, Aaliyah was still stuck, and Matthew hadn't gone to the bathroom yet. I looked at Mr. Harper. The poor guy. He stood there with his arms crossed and a blank, tired, annoyed look on his face. My parents and Mrs. Harper yanked at the door, and we even called over some other skaters to help. I began to believe Aaliyah wasn't making things up. She might really be stuck inside. I tried opening the door, pushing the doorknob down. It eventually became clear that the door wasn't the problem, it was the lock. The lock was indeed broken.

MATTHeW

This trip was not off to a good start. First it was the noisy car ride, then getting woken up at six in the morning to Mom's horrendous singing voice, and now this whole bathroom thing. After Aaliyah had been stuck in the bathroom stall for half an hour, Mom called 911.

I thought about it. I couldn't name one place we'd been to in the past nine exact years where Aaliyah hadn't caused a problem. Dad slapped his head. I could tell he was thinking the exact same thing.

I heard sirens. It was the fire department pulling up.

"Thank goodness you are here!" Mom bellowed. "There is a baby trapped inside the bathroom! MY baby!"

The firemen exchanged looks. "Ma'am? Why would you put a baby in a single stall bathroom alone?" Skaters started gathering around and taking pictures.

"Hey! Don't you dare question me! I am the best parent in the world! Aren't I, Mike?!" Mom yelled at the fire department crew, nudging Dad.

"Yup," Dad muttered under his breath.

I *really* needed to go to the bathroom. I didn't know how long this was going to take. I looked around anxiously, and that's when I noticed Grandma Pearl and Grandma Agnes walking behind the fire truck. Oh no. What were they planning on doing? While everyone was busy trying to get Aaliyah out of the bathroom, they didn't realize that another problem was about to occur. One far, far worse.

Mindy

In the midst of Aaliyah's dilemma, nobody was paying attention to what the actual crazy—or I should say, older and more experienced—people were doing.

The fire truck started moving. Everyone whipped around.

"So long, suckers!" Grandma Agnes screamed out the window. She and Grandma Pearl had taken off in the fire truck! The firemen started chasing them, and the rest of us followed. It was absolute madness! Aaliyah, who was still stuck in the bathroom, started yelling from inside.

"What is going on?! Can someone help me?!"

Aaliyah

I waited in the bathroom for so long that I actually began to worry. I had my doll with me, so at least I could play for a bit. Eventually, though, it wasn't fun anymore.

This was like the time when we were in Hawaii and I had to hide under a bed in the wrong hotel room for three hours—but worse. I was stuck with no way out.

Delaney

Grandma Pearl and Grandma Agnes obviously didn't know how to drive a fire truck. They swerved off the road and drove through a bunch of snowy pine trees before crashing into a massive tree. A pound of snow fell from a branch at the top. Everyone ran over. The firemen pulled the grandmas from the truck and checked them out to make sure they were okay, which they were. The truck, though, had seen better days. The whole front bumper had fallen off, and black smoke started rising. Pretty soon a police car showed up to take Grandma Pearl and Grandma Agnes away. My head raced with questions. Were they going to jail? What was going to happen to Aaliyah?

"Wait! But I have a baby stuck in the bathroom!" Mrs. Harper barked at the cops.

"Ma'am, you'll have to wait. We must call another department to come and get her out. Is your baby walking yet? Or still crawling?" I tried so hard not to laugh when he said that! Mrs. Harper is the weirdest person I've ever met!

"Yeah, she's walking," Mrs. Harper said. She seriously said that. I snorted while trying to hold in my laughter!

Mr. and Mrs. Harper walked back to the hotel to get their car and drive to the police station to bail out the grandmas, or should I say their moms, leaving Cami and my parents in charge of Aaliyah.

A second fire truck pulled up. Ice skaters were taking photos and videos of us crazy people. Matthew still needed to go to the bathroom.

MATTHEW

Once again, more firefighters arrived. I had to go to the bathroom so badly.

That door just wouldn't open. The firefighters tried everything. It got to the point where there weren't any other options but to break down the door! One of the firefighters yelled out to be extra cautious in case the "baby" was near the door.

A firefighter grabbed an ax and carefully cut a little bit of the door away, enough so that they could see her.

"Wait... that's not a baby," the fireman said with a confused and disgusted tone. "That woman told me there was a baby locked inside."

"Yeah, there's no baby. It's just me. I'm nine years old. I wouldn't believe anything she says if I were you," Aaliyah said from inside.

Once the firefighters were done cutting the door down, Aaliyah stepped out and we left to go back to the hotel. We didn't even ice skate once.

* * *

Meanwhile, back at the hotel...

Chicken

This hotel room is amazing! I love ripping apart all the pillows and rolling around in the feathers that burst out of them! And the wood on this bed... WOW, it's so fun to chew! Scratching up all the walls is a very relaxing way to spend the day! I can't wait until my owners and that crazy family get back... they would love to join in on all the fun!

MATTHEW

When we got to the hotel, we were faced with yet another issue. It appeared that Mom, who was supposed to put Chicken in his crate when we left, hadn't done that. Chicken had chewed up everything! And I mean *everything!* Pillows looked like they exploded! There were feathers all over the floor! The carpet and walls were all scratched up! The bedding was torn, and the wooden feet of the beds were bitten up entirely! There was a coffee table in there, too, that had been destroyed and was covered in bite and claw marks. That whole room looked like it had been hit by a tornado. Dad is going to be livid. I don't even want to think about how much this is going to cost in repairs. How could that ball of purple fluff do so much damage?

After finally using the bathroom, I took off my jacket and opened the closet door to put it away. Suddenly, bags of toys and presents came spilling out and bonked my head! Ow! *Why does Aaliyah always get so many cool toys on her birthday, when all I get is socks?* I'm hoping somebody gets me a Turbo Ball 2000 for Christmas. It's the coolest football ever. It's light-weight with a great texture and is fun to throw. I wanted one for my birthday, but of course, Mom and Dad got me socks and a bottle of shampoo.

Grandma Pearl

Agnes and I made some new friends while we were in jail. They were two other ladies, both of them 78 years old, like us—Ethel and Dolores. They live in a nursing home, not far from where Agnes and I live. They'd been arrested for driving with expired license plates. You don't drive much when you live in a nursing home.

Eventually, we all got bailed out and exchanged phone numbers with our new friends. Mike and Tammy were not very happy. They need to lighten up a bit! All we did was drive and crash a firetruck! Sheesh!

Aaliyah

It wasn't until the later part of the evening when Mom, Dad, and the grandmas finally arrived at the hotel. Mr. and Mrs. Emerson were in our room supervising us. After everything they'd just witnessed, they didn't trust leaving us alone. Matthew, Delaney, and Cami were at the table playing cards, and I was sitting on the carpet—or what was left of it—with Mindy, unwrapping my dozens of gifts.

Dad's jaw dropped when he stepped inside.

"What is going on?!" he roared.

 Mom ignored him and smiled at me and Mindy playing on the floor with all my new gifts. "Such a delight to see The Baby enjoying her toys!" Mom danced. Dad was fuming. The hotel manager had come in earlier to discuss the expenses of repairing the room and we had to break the news to dad.

The total estimated cost came out to be a little over $2,000. Dad was going to have to replace all of it—two beds, bedding, a table, part of the carpet, and even a part of the wall that had been scratched up. It was at this point that he just lost it.

"I AM PUTTING MY FOOT DOWN! I'M TIRED OF ALL THIS MISCHIEF! MATTHEW AND CAMILLE, GO TO BED. EMERSONS, GO BACK TO YOUR ROOM. AALIYAH, PUT THESE TOYS AWAY. MOM, PEARL, THAT DOG IS GOING TO THE POUND! TAMMY, WE NEED TO TALK. TOO MUCH HAS HAPPENED IN THESE PAST NINE YEARS AND IT'S TIME FOR THE

PROBLEMS TO STOP." Dad opened the door and the Emersons scrammed. People were coming out of other hotel rooms to take pictures and videos with their phones.

"Okay people, nothing to see here." Dad said and slammed the door shut.

"Tammy, why didn't you put Chicken in his crate? You told me you'd do it when we left!"

"Well, Mike, I didn't know how to lock it. Aww, just look at The Baby! Her eyes are so sparkly!"

Dad was beyond furious now. "Well, if you didn't know how to lock the crate, then instead of leaving that dog unattended for hours, you could have asked for help! Then this would have all been avoided! Instead of avoiding the issue, just say you're sorry! Also, when should we have Aaliyah's birthday cake?"

Oooh! I got excited! Did he say cake?!

Camille

We all needed a break. Mom and Dad decided to get Aaliyah's cake and eat it now, even though it was getting late. I went to the Emerson's room and told them to come over to ours for cake, while Matthew stayed back to keep an eye on the grandmas and Aaliyah. We sat Aaliyah down in a chair at the wooden table that Chicken had chewed up. Then Matthew and I turned off all the lights.

"What's going on?" Aaliyah asked.

Aaliyah

After Dad calmed down, Mindy, Delaney, and their parents came into our room. When Cami and Matthew turned off all the lights, I knew that they were about to bring in the cake, since I'd heard Dad talking about it. I pretended to act surprised, though. So much had already happened, and it was the least I could do to make everyone feel better.

A few minutes later, Mom and Dad came into our room holding the biggest, fanciest, most amazing cake I'd ever seen. It was tall enough to touch the sky! On top of the cake sat nine twinkling candles and a pile of sugared roses.

"Today we honor the most special, most perfect, most angelic, innocent creature that has ever existed in all of history!" Mom shouted at the top of her lungs. The fire on the candles started blowing around just from her voice. *Yikes*. She and Dad put the massive cake in front of me on the table, and everyone began singing "Happy Birthday." Dad opened a drawer in the room's tiny kitchen and brought out utensils and plates.

"Make a wish," Matthew said when he, Cami, and the Emersons stopped singing, Mom and the grandmas stopped shouting, Chicken stopped barking, and Dad stopped lip-syncing.

I wish to find out the truth about Matthew, if he's an alien or not, by the time he leaves to go back to college in a few weeks. I blew out all nine candles, and everyone clapped. After a tough day, it turned out to be a good night and a great cake.

For some reason, it felt like something was missing, though.

That's when I realized that I'd left Mom's expensive designer purse back in the bathroom at the ice-skating pond!

7

Purse Search

Mindy

That was a delicious cake and a great way to end the night. We had just made it back to our room when I heard knocking at our door. Mommy and Daddy were busy talking to Delaney about different boyfriend options, so I answered. Aaliyah was standing there looking nervous.

"Mindy! I need your help," she whispered. "Remember that white and gold purse my mom gave me this morning? Well, I lost it. *Please* help me find it. My Dad is going to flip." I hesitated, not knowing what I'd be able to do about it. Plus, I didn't want to get in trouble.

"Mindy, please." Aaliyah gave me puppy eyes, and I couldn't resist helping my best friend.

"Okay. I'll help you. What's the plan?"

Delaney

"I'll be back soon. Aaliyah and I are just going downstairs to get some hot chocolate from the dispenser in the lobby," Mindy announced. Mom and Dad ignored her, but I knew something had to be up. I mean, just based on who she was with. Honestly, Mindy's not that bad of a kid in general, but put her with Aaliyah and her behavior totally shifts. It's almost like Aaliyah's energy and bad choices rub off on Mindy.

"Look at this one, Delaney. I found another dating website that might work." Dad shoved his phone in my face to show me the site. Wow, he desperately wants me and Matthew to break up. For a moment I forgot about Aaliyah and Mindy as I told him that mine and Matthew's relationship wasn't going anywhere and I didn't want to hear it. When I looked back up, the door was closed, and Mindy and Aaliyah were gone.

MATTHEW

Aaliyah and Mindy had said they were going to get hot chocolate, but that couldn't be the case. It was past 9:00 p.m. Why would they be getting hot chocolate after eating a ton of cake? Even after we had cake, the craziness continued. After about an hour, Mom noticed Aaliyah still wasn't back. She panicked and called 911. Again. It just doesn't end.

Aaliyah

Mindy and I put on our warm coats and walked back to the frozen pond we were at earlier in the day. It wasn't too far, only about a block away. When we got to the broken bathroom stall, the door had a taped sign on it that said "Closed for Repairs." I opened the door anyway and found the purse still there, but it was completely covered in ice! The water bottle I had placed inside of it this morning had leaked everywhere, freezing not just the purse, but my doll! I was worried the gold chain would rust and the leather would be ruined. I would get in huge trouble for ruining Mom's expensive purse!

While walking back to the hotel with the purse trying to figure out how to fix the problem, we heard sirens so we ran. What if there was a criminal on the loose?

Camille

My parents and I got into the police car and started driving around, looking for Aaliyah and Mindy. The sirens blared right above my head. Matthew had gone over to Mr. and Mrs. Emerson's room to fill them in. What an eventful day it has been! The only good thing that happened was that Matthew didn't seem afraid of Chicken anymore. I was happy he was facing his fears. Chicken is so small and cute; nobody could ever really fear him.

Dad was so infuriated that his breathing was heavy. The police officer asked him if he needed an ambulance.

"I'm fine. Just angry," Dad grunted.

I honestly didn't blame him. I, myself, was angry. Very, very angry. I was angry that we could never do anything as a family without having a problem. I was angry that every time I returned home from college, nobody seemed to have missed me. I was angry with Aaliyah, Grandma Pearl, Grandma Agnes, Mindy, and with Mom. Especially Mom. She's always treated people so unfairly! It's like the only two people in the whole world she cares about are Aaliyah and herself! She never ever asks me, Matthew, or Dad about our lives. She never asks *anyone* how they're doing! She only ever talks about herself and her "incredible baby." It's all about Mom and Aaliyah. Forget about Camille, forget about Matthew, forget about Dad, the Emersons, or people in public who aren't doing anything wrong. It's just "Stuff stuff stuff! Me me me! Aaliyah Aaliyah Aaliyah!"

Mom has been like this for as long as I could remember. Even before Aaliyah came along, Mom was very self-centered. Aaliyah just happened to make things worse. I've never said anything about this to Mom, though. I've never talked to her about how I feel. The only person I've ever talked to was Matthew, who feels the same way. Other than that, I've always kept quiet and tried to be nice, but after twenty-one years, I've finally reached my breaking point. I cannot take it anymore. She is unfair and downright selfish, and I am sick of it!

Aaliyah

We got back to the hotel. Disaster avoided! Mindy and I went to my room. The rest of my family wasn't there. Grandma Pearl and Grandma Agnes were gone, too. I felt relieved, but why would everyone leave the hotel this late at night? I got suspicious but shook it off. They'd be back so I better hurry and fix Mom's purse. I put the purse in the microwave and set it for five minutes. That would sure warm it up!

Mindy

We were able to find the purse, but then Aaliyah came up with a "smart" idea. She put it in the microwave. For FIVE minutes! What was she thinking?! I tried talking her out of it, but she said that her dad would be very mad and she felt bad for him. I decided to let her do what she wanted. With Aaliyah, it's always "my way or the highway." The moment she decides on something, there's no changing her mind. She put the purse in the microwave, set it for five minutes, and hit the start button.

The purse started zapping around in the microwave. I peered through the see-through door to see the plastic on the doll melting and the leather of the purse bubbling. There were popping sounds. The only popping that should come from a microwave is popcorn! A horrible smell started seeping from the microwave. Everything went from too cold to too hot, too fast!

"Aaliyah, we should probably take it out now!" I tried telling her, but Aaliyah told me that she microwaves food all the time, so a purse should be no different. I just knew that sooner or later, disaster was going to occur. We heard barking coming from under the bed and saw Chicken's purple face peering out from under it. He had the right idea by hiding. I was wishing I could do the same because I knew trouble was coming.

Sparks continued to fly inside the microwave. The purse exploded! Aaliyah and I jumped back, as the microwave door busted open, and sparks and black smoke flew everywhere! Suddenly, the smoke detector started blaring loudly above our heads. We heard dozens of footsteps outside the door. Aaliyah cracked it open to see what was going on. People had started running out of their rooms, holding their belongings thinking they needed to evacuate because of a fire. *Well Aaliyah, now your dad is going to be REALLY mad, coming back to his hotel room to find this mess. Much madder than if he saw a frozen purse.*

The purse—or what was left of it—tumbled out of the microwave. The doll was completely gone... other than her hair, which was floating in a puddle of melted plastic. So much for Aaliyah's "smart" idea. Meh. It's not my problem.

MATTHEW

As I walked around the hotel with Delaney and her parents looking for Mindy and Aaliyah, we heard the shrieking sound of a smoke detector. I stopped in my tracks, closed my eyes, and shook my head. I knew it had something to do with Aaliyah. We followed the sound back to my family's hotel room. Outside, people were walking around with their belongings, confused. Some were asking if they needed to evacuate.

Just like I had predicted, Aaliyah, Mindy, and Chicken were in our room. There was a wretched smell of melted plastic and the air was filled with smoke. The girls were standing in the small kitchen with a guilty look on their faces. Aaliyah, Mindy, and Chicken looked like they'd rubbed themselves against car tires. The microwave looked like it had been set on fire. There was ash everywhere. We called Mom, Dad, and Cami to tell them we found the girls and to come back to the hotel and they showed up a few minutes later.

"Oh, good! The Baby is here!" Mom squealed running into the room with Dad, Cami, and a police officer following behind.

I glanced behind me at Dad. He did not look amused. "I leave for ten minutes and already you guys have destroyed something?! As if I haven't spent enough money and time!"

Oh, for crying out loud! None of us had gotten a minute of sleep yet and tomorrow we are supposed to go to the Grand Canyon! This night didn't seem to have an end.

Grandma Pearl

While everyone else was fighting about where our granddaughter was or wasn't, Agnes and I snuck off. Our new friends from jail, Ethel and Dolores, wanted to get together and gossip.

8

Grandma Patrol

Camille

The manager of the hotel needed to come to our room again due to the whole microwave incident. He also had to explain to all the shaken guests outside with their belongings that it was a false alarm.

"TWO HUNDRED DOLLARS????!!!!!!!!!!!!!!" Dad yelled. He was so mad, he stomped his foot down and accidentally tripped over Chicken's crate, landing right on his wrist. "OUCH!"

Next thing I knew, I was driving my parents to the emergency room because Dad might have broken his wrist.

They should check his blood pressure and heart rate, too, I thought to myself. He was probably on the verge of having a heart attack at this point due to his anger levels.

When Mom, Dad, and I arrived at the hospital, Dad was immediately taken in for an X-ray. That left just me and Mom in the waiting room. I decided I needed to tell her how I felt. If she got mad at me, then let her. After all these years, I needed to get it out.

"You need to be nicer to people. It's embarrassing when you yell at someone and cause a scene in public. And Aaliyah needs to learn how to follow directions better! Why can't you just tell her to cut the drama and be a normal kid?"

Mom stared at me blankly. I think she was failing to understand the point.

I tried to explain myself again. "What I mean is… why do you treat Aaliyah like a baby? You never treated Matthew or I like babies," I said.

"Okay fine. I will try harder," Mom promised. I took that as a good sign, even if I wasn't sure she was being serious.

After several hours of being stuck in the waiting room and dozing on the most uncomfortable chairs ever, Dad's X-Ray results came back. He hadn't broken his wrist. It was just sprained and bruised. The doctor placed Dad's wrist in a stretchy bandage. Mom had gone to the gift shop "to get a snack," and I sat outside with Dad, drawing little pictures on his new bandage.

Mom eventually came out of the gift shop, almost toppling over with bags full of toys.

"Tammy! Why did you just buy all these useless toys?" Dad snapped. "And don't buy another purse, either. What did you expect would happen, lending it to Aaliyah? The girl can't even remember to put on sunscreen when playing on a beach in Hawaii for two hours!"

"What, Mikey-poo? I just got The Babies new toys and some bedtime stories to read to my three children!" The Bab*ies*? *Three* children? Mikey-poo? I started to wonder if talking to Mom about how she should love us more was a bad idea.

Tammy Harper

I didn't completely understand what Camille was talking about at the hospital. I mean, The Baby *is* the queen of all life and existence, but if it makes my family happier, then I will start giving Mike, Camille, and Matthew the same attention I give to The Baby!

Aaliyah

I was sound asleep when Mom's blaring voice woke me up.

"Baby #2! Let's read a bedtime story!" She was leaning over Matthew who was asleep on the couch.

Matthew opened his eyes and gave her an angry look. Why did she just call him 'Baby #2?'

"Mom, I am not in the mood for jokes right now." I could tell he was confused. I was, too. Why would Mom call him Baby #2 or want to read to him, let alone give him any attention at all?

MATTHEW

Mom wasn't acting right when they got home from the hospital. She woke me up with her booming voice. She brought in bags that were filled with toys. There were race cars, action figures, and stuffed animals. Turns out, the toys were for me and Cami. None of them were for Aaliyah, though. I thanked Mom, even though I thought it was the biggest waste of money. Weirdest of all, she kept on calling me "The Baby #2" and Cami "The Baby #3." She was also calling Dad "Mikey-poo." It was pretty horrific.

Whatever. I just wanted to go back to sleep. I noticed it was very quiet. Too quiet. And then I realized I couldn't hear Grandma Pearl and Grandma Agnes snoring in the attached room. I couldn't even remember the last time I saw them... WAIT— THEY WERE MISSING!

Camille

There is never a dull moment around here. Five minutes after arriving back at the hotel from the hospital, Mom panicked and called 911. Again. The grandmas were nowhere to be found.

Sheriff Campbell, Arizona P.D.

In just twenty-four hours, my department has received several calls for help from the same family. Twenty-four hours! This is highly unacceptable.

There are much more serious emergencies to deal with than helping these maniacs with whatever it is they are calling about. Everyone in my department agrees.

MATTHEW

As if this night wasn't already bad enough, the police showed up to search for Grandma Pearl and Grandma Agnes. They were not happy.

"This is the third time we've seen each other, and it hasn't even been twenty-four hours. You need to understand that we have other emergencies. Please try to be more cautious so that we can help the citizens who truly need us," Sheriff Campbell said, looking flustered and angry.

Mom got mad. Real mad. "We have elderly family members missing! What is wrong with you?!" she hissed at him and the other officer. These poor guys.

Aaliyah

The police officers and my parents left to search for Grandma Pearl and Grandma Agnes. I was tired from not sleeping enough, but I wanted to help, too. I quietly left the room. I swore an oath that for the rest of this trip, I'd be on Grandma Patrol. I wouldn't let them out of my sight.

As I searched the halls for any signs of my grandmas, I was also thinking about Matthew. I still hadn't proven my theory about him being an alien. I honestly want to go home. Not only because this trip stunk, but also because I want to record him some more. I need to know his secret. My mission hasn't been accomplished!

Delaney

"Yes, we will be there as soon as possible," Mom whispered into the phone. According to Mrs. Harper, Grandma Pearl and Grandma Agnes had gone missing. She needed our help looking for them. It was starting to look like the Grand Canyon would have to wait.

While Dad and Mindy slept, Mom and I made our way down the hallways throughout the hotel.

Suddenly, I heard old-lady voices. They were coming from around the corner. I walked toward the sound and turned the corner to find the grandmas and a few other senior citizens playing cards, eating hard caramel candy, and gossiping!

"Hello there, young missy," Grandma Pearl said. "Aren't you my grandson's girlfriend?"

"Um yeah, haha," I said awkwardly. "Sorry to interrupt you, but I think Mr. and Mrs. Harper need you back—"

"Oh Pearl, you're right. Marriage is only for adults," Grandma Agnes said, cutting me off. Um, MARRIAGE? We aren't married! We're too young to get married!

One of the other ladies shook her head and sighed. "Today I want you to take your boyfriend outside and leave him out there so that he takes the hint that you're not interested," she said, pointing a bony, wrinkly finger at me.

"Children these days. They date each other like their lives depend on it! Like, how old are you, honey bunches, twelve?"

I couldn't believe she just said that to me! Old people have no filter!

"Actually, I'm eighteen." I looked them in the eyes. They all gasped.

Another lady agreed. "Tsk tsk tsk. This is another problem with modern day children. They eat candy instead of fruits and vegetables, so they end up being short! They look much younger than they are!"

Wow. She actually said that to me! What is her deal?! First of all, I am over a head taller than all of them. I'm even a little taller than Matthew! I couldn't see how they'd think I'm short. Second of all, candy isn't what makes people short. In fact, candy has nothing to do with height at all. Third of all, I don't eat that much junk food. Fourth of all, I'm not getting married for a long, long time. Fifth of all, they don't get to decide who I date or disrespect my decisions. Sixth of all, it's not their place to tell me what to do about Matthew. I don't even think they know my name. Seventh of all, I love Matthew and his grandmas should, too. It's not nice to say those things about him. And finally, eighth of all, they were the ones sitting on the floor eating candy. If candy is *that* bad, then why were they eating it?

I called Mrs. Harper from my cell phone to let her know we found the grandmas. Mom came around the corner just in time to help me get the grandmas back to their hotel room, but not before they exchanged phone numbers and addresses with all their new friends. This couldn't possibly be good.

Aaliyah

I walked around the whole hotel, but there was no sign of the grandmas. I took a detour and ended up in the laundry room. I wasn't there long when I heard footsteps and whistling walking towards the room, so I climbed up some boxes, jumped inside the linen cart, and buried myself in sheets so they wouldn't see me. Ew! The sheets smelled just as bad as Matthew's armpits!

All of a sudden, the cart started moving. Where were we going? Was I going to be stuck in here for hours? I was going to be in so much trouble!

9

Kicked Out

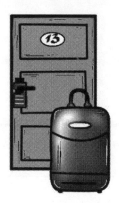

Janitor Sonny

Just as my early morning shift started, I was wheeling the linen cart to the laundry room. I thought I saw it moving a bit. I shook it off, thinking I needed more coffee.

I wheeled the cart to the washing machine and started taking things out. When I reached the bottom, I figured out why the linen was moving. To my surprise, there was a young girl hiding underneath the sheets.

MATTHEW

The hotel manager knocked on our door. Mom answered and he told her the latest news.

"We got a report from our custodian. There was a little girl in the linen cart, with auburn hair and wearing pajamas. She told him that she had been separated from her family and was really scared. I feel like I may have seen her with you guys before?" He looked at us suspiciously, like he already knew that she was with us. I slapped my forehead. We were so busy dealing with all the grandma drama, none of us noticed Aaliyah was gone. Her bed looked like she was in it with all the pillows. Typical BBLS thing.

"Yes, she's ours!" Mom yelped.

The manager scrunched up his face at the sound. "Okay, ma'am you must come to the front desk. She is waiting down there. Please keep a better eye on her. We are busy working, and you need to watch her so it won't happen again."

Although he said it politely and was absolutely right, Mom got offended like she always does. "Excuse me?! What did you just say?! The Baby is a perfect little creature! She would never do anything harmful! 'Keep a better eye on her.' Give me a break! She is beyond perfect! How dare you talk to me that way? You better believe I will call the police and shut down this entire place!" She got all up in his face, shouting at him.

The manager quickly left, and before we knew it, not one, not two, but three police cars arrived at the hotel. Not for the manager, but to talk to Mom about what she'd been saying. It was the manager who had called them. I was so humiliated!

I went with Delaney to the front desk to pick up Aaliyah. Dad came down to talk to us.

"Matthew, Aaliyah, come to the room and pack your bags. We've been booted."

I looked at him with wide eyes. "Wait, what? Why are we kicked out of the hotel? What are we going to do now?" I asked. Delaney looked worried, and Aaliyah looked curious.

"Your mom has gotten us kicked out. The new plan is to go visit the Grand Canyon today with Delaney and her family and then leave for home straight from there." He had an angry look on his face. I caught my reflection in the mirror and noticed I did, too.

Jim, Arizona Canyon Hotel Manager

In the twenty years I've been working here, this is the most annoying family I have ever dealt with.

Aaliyah

When I was taken over to the front desk, I could tell I was about to be in a lot of trouble, so I tried acting innocent.

"I've been separated from my family. I am cold, alone, and afraid." I gave the manager my puppy eyes. I feel like every time I use the Puppy Eyes Method, I always end up getting what I want. Kind of like how I convinced Mindy to come with me to the pond to retrieve the purse.

"Okay kid, we will do what we can," the manager said softly, and gave me a pitiful look. It worked! I tried to keep a straight face. I nearly laughed so hard!

After a few minutes of waiting for the manager to "locate" my family, he came back with a very angry look on his face and a clenched jaw. Matthew and Delaney came to the lobby to get me. Suddenly, behind them Dad showed up and said we've been kicked out of the hotel and needed to leave. He told us what Mom said to the manager. I got mad at Mom! I stopped to think about it. Although Mom's meltdown contributed, I don't think we're getting kicked out just because of that. Since we got here, we've been causing trouble.

Dad needed to pay for all the damages. It came out to over $2,300 for repairs on all the things we destroyed—the furniture in one room and the microwave in the other. He also needed to pay another $650 for our stay itself. He was so mad he couldn't even look at us.

"Where is Mom? I need to talk to her," I said.

"She's outside the building talking to the police for the fourth time this trip," Dad said.

I was furious! Mom was giving us all a bad reputation! Going home wasn't entirely bad, though. I could continue spying on Matthew and complete my mission!

10

Breaking News!

Delaney

Apparently, the Harpers have been booted from the hotel. What else is new? I am so annoyed. It might be time to start looking into the dating websites Mom and Dad shared with me. Better yet, maybe I need to be single for a while.

After checking out of the hotel, we drove to the Grand Canyon. The view was spectacular and I couldn't wait to explore. I also couldn't help but feel a little nervous. This place seemed like a playground for troublemakers. We parked, then took a bus down to a fast, strong-flowing river. Things got so bad from there on. Like, SO bad!

MATTHEW

Down by the river at the base of the Grand Canyon, we sort of just split into two groups. Delaney, her parents, Cami, Dad, and me went to check out one area, while Mom, the grandmas, Mindy, Aaliyah, and Chicken stayed with each other. In hindsight, why did we let all the troublemakers stick together?

MIKE HARPER

My wrist wrap is itchy.

Aaliyah

There was a raft tied to a log on the river. Grandma Agnes and Grandma Pearl exchanged mischievous grins.

"Aaliyah, will you hold Chicken for me?" Grandma Agnes asked.

I take the purple dog, not really thinking about it. I really should have, though...

Camille

I never should've talked to Mom about being nice. She doesn't know how. I don't like being called "The Baby #3," and Matthew doesn't like being called "The Baby #2," but more than ever, Dad despises being called "Mikey-poo." Now I had a glimpse of how Aaliyah has felt her entire life. We all agreed that we liked the old Mom better, when the rest of us didn't have to deal with her. Just Aaliyah.

At the Grand Canyon, while we normal people were off looking around, apparently the not-so-normal ones decided to take a ride on a river raft that didn't even belong to them.

Mindy

"Come on! Get on the raft, young children!" Grandma Pearl and Grandma Agnes were telling Aaliyah and me. Mrs. Harper was sitting in the front, putting on makeup. Man did I luck out with my mommy. I don't know what I'd do if she was like Mrs. Harper.

We got onto the raft, put on the life jackets that were sitting in the seats, and untied the rope from the log that was holding it in place. The raft slowly started to drift down the river. Mrs. Harper dropped a tube of lipstick in the cold water.

"My lipstick!" she cried. Tourists turned to stare.

Our raft floated toward a tree on the side of the river and hit one of its branches. The branch was so sharp that it tore a large hole on the side of the raft. Aaliyah, who was holding Chicken, went tumbling into the river!

"THE BABY!" Mrs. Harper screamed. We looked back. Aaliyah and Chicken were bobbing in the water but seemed to be okay. I couldn't tell if Mrs. Harper was more worried about Aaliyah or about her lipstick.

"MY RAFT!" Someone yelled.

I really hope this doesn't cause a huge commotion. I crossed my fingers. But the current started to get stronger, and none of us knew what to do or how to control the raft, which had slowly started to deflate from hitting the branch. Chicken and Aaliyah were not far behind us, also being pushed by the current.

A few minutes later, a river rescue crew showed up in a boat. They were going to save us!

A voice blared through a megaphone. *"On the raft, it looks like two senior citizens, along with a little girl and a woman putting on makeup and taking selfies. In the water is another little girl who is holding onto a purple stuffed animal."*

The boat came up behind us, and one of the crew members leaned over to grab onto our raft. I thought he was going to fall in! He attached a rope so they could tow us to safety. Another crew member threw out a life float for Chicken and Aaliyah.

"Grab on!" he yelled. "Wait—that purple thing is alive?!"

Aaliyah

I was shivering. That water was like ice! I grabbed onto the life float and me and Chicken were lifted into the rescue boat. Chicken started barking. He barks awfully loud, considering he's only about five pounds.

"Hey kid, is that a wind-up toy? Or is it actually alive?!" one of the rescue crew guys asked as he gave me a towel.

"Yup, it's real," I said. My lips were numb from the cold water. I wondered what Dad was doing right now. He is not going to be happy about this one.

The rescue crew safely brought the raft and the rest of our group back to shore. We were going to have to trudge all the way back to the starting point to meet the rest of our family.

"Are you sure that's a dog?" the rescue crew guy asked me again. "I mean, it's a bit of a… um, unusual color."

"I don't even know at this point," I said.

Mom went into teaching mode. "Aaliyah little sweetness, what does the dog say? The dog says 'woof!'" she yelped. The entire rescue crew gave her weirded-out looks.

I was so relieved to be back on dry land, but the adventure wasn't over when we got to the rest of our group.

MATTHEW

Are Mindy and my family always up to no good? Yes. But has it ever gotten to the point of a newscast? No. Well, not until today.

While their group was being rescued, a television news crew showed up! They interviewed Dad first.

"Sir, what do you have to say about this unfortunate incident?" the reporter asked.

"Mhm," Dad mumbled. I looked over his shoulder and saw Cami and Delaney's parents hiding behind a bush.

"Sir, can you repeat that?" he asked Dad.

"Mhm."

"Can we get closed captioning?" the reporter called out to another TV crew member. I couldn't wait until it was my turn to be interviewed!

Mindy

"Wow, that is the weirdest looking dog I've ever seen," I heard one of our rescuers whisper to another.

When we got back to our starting point, there were literally news reporters filming! I've always wanted to be on the news, so it was like a dream come true! I jumped in front of the camera, which was interviewing Matthew, and waved hi.

"Hello America! Mindy Emerson here, reporting from the Grand Canyon!" I yelled as loud as I could at the camera. I was going to be on TV! I needed to make a good impression!

"Get out of the way, Mindy!" Matthew whispered harshly at me, trying to continue with his interview. "My little sister has also done stuff to me such as 'Punch Me' signs. But worse! When we were in Hawaii over the summer for my birthday, she put a stencil that said 'Punch Me' on my back while I was lying in the sun. So, I ended up getting a 'Punch Me' tan line! ON MY BIRTHDAY!"

I looked at Aaliyah, wondering if what Matthew was saying was true. She nodded her head proudly.

The newscasters weren't the only ones filming. Tourists everywhere were recording on their phones.

The rescue crew unloaded the deflated raft, and an angry bystander, who I'm guessing was the owner of that raft, stomped over to us.

"Hey! Which one of you fools is going to give me $700 to replace my raft?!" he exploded.

Mrs. Harper chimed in. "Oh yes, my husband Mikey-poo would be honored!" The intrigued news reporter turned the camera in their direction to film them. This trip has been such a disaster.

Delaney

Well, that was interesting. Mr. Harper paid the $700 and yelled at Aaliyah, Mindy, Mrs. Harper, Chicken, and the grandmas for the next ten minutes. I really hope that someday he gets a break from them. He desperately needs one.

The Harpers needed to leave for home that day, since they had gotten kicked out of the hotel. We decided to leave, too. The only reason we went on this trip was for Aaliyah.

Mindy wanted to drive with the Harpers to be with Aaliyah, and Cami and Matthew decided to ride in our car to get away from her. There was no space left in our car for anyone else to come, so that left Mr. Harper alone in the car with the troublemakers and no other ally.

Aaliyah

Dad's arm hurt too much to drive, so Mom had to drive us instead. Dad is a pretty angry person, but you haven't seen *true* anger until you've seen Mom behind the wheel of a car. She has the worst road rage on Planet Earth.

Mike Harper

No words are strong enough to describe my immense headache throughout the most horrid drive of my life.

Aaliyah

There was major traffic when we reached the city. Mom got angry and rolled down her window to scream at the driver in front of us.

"IT'S CALLED A GAS PEDAL, LADY! A DYING TURTLE IS FASTER THAN YOU! MOVE IT! I HAVE A BABY IN THE CAR WHO MUST GET HOME!" She pressed down on the car horn. Since nobody was moving, people started getting out of their cars to ask her what the deal was. It was crazy!

"There is a baby in my car. Like, you guys need to learn how to drive! Like, are you like, fifteen years old and just learning how?! Like, don't you have a license?!" Mom screamed at everyone, pointing her finger with great force, and waving her arms around in the air. People started looking into our car and were giving us angry looks. I hid my face out of embarrassment.

"Well, what do you want me to do? Nobody here is moving, am I supposed to bash into all these other cars and cause an accident? Then you *really* won't be getting home!" a guy yelled out his window. I have to admit, he's right.

"Are you sure you have a baby? I don't see a baby in there." Some lady was literally staring into our car, her face pressed against my window. The grandmas rolled down their windows and made growling noises at people. Chicken bared his teeth.

"Is that supposed to be a dog? Why is it purple?" the woman looking into our car asked. She pulled out her phone to take a picture of Chicken.

I looked at the floor and saw Dad lying down there, desperately trying to not be seen. His method didn't work, though, because someone else stuck their head through the window and asked, "Hey, is that a human lying down there?! BODY! IT'S A DEAD BODY!" Dad had no choice but to look up and let the freaked-out person know that he's very much alive.

Seconds later, other drivers started rolling down *their* windows and yelling. "WHAT ARE YOU ALL DOING?! THE ROAD IS NOW OPEN!" Everyone rolled their eyes and got back in their cars. Dad was still slumped down on the floor of the car.

Eventually, we dropped off Mindy at her house and finally made it back home. What happened there was even more horrifying.

MATTHEW

I was glad I got to drive with Delaney instead of my own family this time.

When I got home, Dad was slumped on Grandma Pearl's bed, which was where the couch used to be. He groaned and turned on the TV. The first thing on the screen was the news... and there I was! At the Grand Canyon talking about my 'Punch Me' tan line to the camera while Aaliyah and Chicken were busy getting rescued! *Breaking news! The*

Grand Canyon rescue crew saves a group of tourists who went for a joy ride on a stolen raft!"

While we were watching my interview, Grandma Pearl and Grandma Agnes decided to leave the house and go for a walk without telling us.

11

Chicken & Rooster

Aaliyah

I couldn't believe my eyes. I was on the news! I sure hope all the kids in my class are watching this! I'm famous!

We heard a ring at the door. It was Grandma Pearl and Grandma Agnes. Had they gone for a walk?

Turns out, the grandmas weren't the only ones at the door.

"BAAAARRRRKKKKKKKK!!!!!!"

"AAAAAAAAAHHHHHHHHHH!!!!"

There was a terrifying dog with razor-sharp teeth that was bigger than me! It was all ratty and hairy and had huge claws and a collar with spikes coming out of it! Matthew screamed, ran to the kitchen, and jumped onto a countertop, knocking over an open box of cereal! The giant dog started eating the cereal, which had spilled everywhere. We all stood frozen.

"Do you like Rooster? We found him behind a gate," Grandma Agnes said. Matthew was pale and shivering. Chicken looked happy to have a friend. Dad was sleeping through all of it, with the news story of us on the river raft still playing in the background.

"I'll go to the supermarket to get some new cereal. We need groceries anyway," Mom said, and my anxiety skyrocketed. Oh no! Who knows what she's *actually* planning on getting over there, and Dad wasn't awake to tell her not to go!

MATTHEW

Matthew, this is your life we're talking about here. This is your LIFE in your hands. There were no hiding places nearby, and that monster was looking me straight in the eye. There were no options but to sprint. I had never been more scared. The beast was getting closer. And Mom... was going to the store.

Aaliyah

An hour passed. Mom was still at the store. Matthew never got off the countertop. We heard the doorbell ring. Chicken and Rooster started howling and running to the front door.

"HEY! THAT'S OUR DOG! YOU THIEVES!" There was a young couple with purple and blue hair, nose piercings, and heavy makeup standing at our front door.

"It's our Rooster, you modern day children!" Grandma Pearl sneered at them, spit flying from her mouth.

"We went outside to let our dog, Princess, inside and she was missing! We've been going around the neighborhood asking if anyone has seen her. She couldn't have gotten out! The fence door was closed tightly like always," the girl explained.

Grandma Agnes started making hissing noises at them. The couple stared at her in confusion and disbelief.

"Wait..." the boy began. "Aren't you the people who were just on the news for stealing a raft and having to be rescued in the Grand Canyon? That's what we were watching before we went to let Princess in."

"Yeah," I said. "That's us. I'm famous! Would you like an autograph?"

I heard Dad snoring on the couch and saw Cami burying her face in pillows with embarrassment. Matthew was still on the countertop. Just then, Mom got back home from her trip to "get cereal." There was a huge truck along with her.

"Steady, you guys! You're very strong!" Mom was screeching at a bunch of men who were hauling a TV!

"Tammy!" Dad woke up and shouted.

Camille

I got up to watch the drama unfold. This was like something out of Mom's soap operas!

"We don't need a new TV! The one we have is just fine!" Dad said desperately. The workers carrying in the TV looked so intrigued. *So much for getting cereal,* I thought.

"No Mikey-poo, this TV isn't for us. I got it to put in The Baby #1's room!"

Dad's jaw dropped. "WHAT?! Do you realize this TV is nicer than ours? A LOT nicer than ours? Aaliyah doesn't even need a TV to begin with!"

"Well, Mikey-poo, she deserves it. She is such an overachiever! And besides, The Baby #1 has such a kind soul that she'd share with you and Babies #2 and #3."

Aaliyah started jumping around and clapping her hands, talking about how excited she was to watch her princess shows on the new TV. Matthew hadn't come down from the counter. Mom squealed with glee over "how cute The Baby is." I really am the only normal one in my family.

Aaliyah

Once Mom and Dad's fight broke out, Princess's (or Rooster's) owners thought it'd be best to skedaddle. They grabbed their dog when the grandmas weren't looking and ran.

"FOUR THOUSAND DOLLARS?!" Dad gasped when one of the delivery guys handed him the receipt. "AND AN EXTRA NINE HUNDRED FOR THE INSTALLATION?!" Dad told the guys who were putting up the TV that he'd like to return it, but we found out there was nothing he could do about it.

"We're sorry sir, but our store is shutting down in three days and everything is final sale. We're not taking returns." It was from the same store as the grandmas' furniture! Dad's jaw was opened wide enough to fit in an entire apple.

"Fine! Then I'll sell it! Just like all the other random, worthless furniture that's sitting in our living room!" He threw his hands up in the air and yelled. "Just finish putting up the TV and get out of my house!" Dad stomped upstairs to his room, slamming the door behind him.

Pretty soon, my TV was up and working! Right on the wall across from my bed, too, so I could watch TV in bed at night! I felt bad for Dad, but I loved my new TV more!

I went to bed excited that night. Well actually, I didn't go to bed. I was up watching TV. I wasn't excited about just the TV, though. We'll be getting a Christmas tree tomorrow, and, best of all, Grandma Pearl and Grandma Agnes are leaving for a few weeks and won't be back until Christmas!

Mike Harper

All I wanted was to watch basketball.

12

Destruction on Aisle Nine

Camille

The next day, which I thought would finally be calmer since the grandmas were leaving, was the craziest one yet, if that was even possible.

It started when we left to buy our tree in the morning.

MATTHEW

Aaliyah opened the door to my room and walked in. Why does she never knock?!

"How does it feel to be nine?" I asked her.

"Exactly the same. Hey Matthew, what do you do at college?" She looked suspicious. What was she up to?

"Well, you go to class, you have a lot of work, I dunno. It's stressful, but fun."

"Do you ever..." she began.

"Yeah?"

Aaliyah leaned in and whispered, "Matthew. I know your secret. I promise I won't tell anyone about the aliens."

"Huh? What secret? What aliens?" Oh boy. What was she up to this time? I yelled at Aaliyah to get out of my room.

"That's my name!" she yelled back. She's said that every single time someone said her name since the day she could talk. It drives me crazy. Crazy!

Whatever. This was going to be a good week; I could already tell. The grandmas were leaving, we were going to decorate for Christmas, and Aaliyah would be at school for the next three weeks up until Christmas break!

We left to the hardware store to get our tree. Aaliyah rolled up a piece of paper to make a fake telescope. She was really freaking me out! She held it up to her eye and stared at me through it. On the side of the "telescope," Aaliyah had written **"the mathew mayking theery."** What was all of this supposed to mean? What was she doing? Why did she keep watching me? Also, when will she finally learn how to spell?

Aaliyah

I wanted to see if Matthew would confess his secret, but he didn't. I set up the camcorder on the balcony outside his window so that he wouldn't see it this time. I was planning to leave it up for the day and all night, then collect it when Matthew left his room in the morning.

We went downstairs to say goodbye to Chicken and the grandmas. I gave them hugs and acted all sad for them to be gone, but in reality, I was relieved. I could tell everyone was. Especially Dad.

When Grandma Pearl kissed the top of my head, my hair got stuck in her dentures! Yuck! Mom had to get a pair of scissors to cut them out. Matthew laughed like it was the funniest thing ever.

We left to go to the tree lot at our local hardware store while the grandmas packed up their belongings. I looked up at Matthew's balcony as we pulled out of the driveway and saw the camcorder facing his window. I couldn't wait until tomorrow morning to check the footage!

MATTHEW

When we got to the hardware store, Aaliyah had to go to the bathroom. Mom forced me to take her since Aaliyah "didn't know where it was." I rolled my eyes. She probably just wanted to check out the place.

We started walking to the bathroom, and I called it! Aaliyah *was* just curious and wanted to explore! She even admitted it! We walked down aisle nine. The shelves were cool. They had rows and rows of Christmas ornaments. There was a very tall red ladder that looked like a staircase. It went up to the ceiling to reach things on the top shelf.

"Come on, Matthew! Let's go check it out!" Aaliyah said excitedly.

"No way! We aren't allowed on that!"

"Just admit it, you little goody two shoes. You're dying to climb it." I did have to admit, I was interested. Aaliyah looked around to make sure there were no employees in the aisle and started climbing the ladder. She looked at me and waved for me to come up, but I stayed down.

"You should get down. It isn't safe, and if an employee sees you, they'll get mad," I called up to her.

"So what? It's not like *Mom* will be mad! And all Dad will do is yell for a couple of seconds and then go back to sleep! You know I'm right."

I knew she was right. It wasn't about getting yelled at or in trouble, though. The fact that we were going to make an employee's job harder was not okay. We needed to think about how they'd feel having to stop what they were doing to tell us to get down. It was breaking the rules. So, I stayed down while Aaliyah continued to climb up.

Camille

Mom, Dad, and I looked at a few different trees while waiting for Matthew and Aaliyah to come back. We had to bug an employee to put a bunch of trees on hold, because Mom declared we weren't going to buy anything without "The Baby #1's" approval.

After a while, Matthew and Aaliyah were still not back.

"Baby #3! Go check on them!" Mom shouted in my ear. People looked over at us.

"Okay, okay. Jeez." I went into the store.

Aaliyah

I kept climbing the staircase ladder, getting higher with each step. It was so cool! There were stacks of boxes and all sorts of different Christmas tree ornaments and hardware equipment on shelves going up to the ceiling!

Matthew, the perfect little boy, "didn't want to break the rules." HAHAHAHAHA! How boring!

I reached the top step. Matthew was yelling at me to come down.

"In a second," I called. I was enjoying the view. I could see through the open doors. Mom and Dad were arguing outside with several trees lined up next to them. I could see Cami walking into the store looking irritated. I reached out and grabbed a box of sparkling colorful Christmas ornaments. I knew Mom would buy them for me if I asked.

The heavy box wasn't coming out, so I kept tugging. And then, and only then, did I start to panic like never before.

Camille

There was a huge commotion coming from aisle nine. I was almost one hundred percent certain I knew who the culprits were.

I went over to see what all the noise was about, and oh my goodness me...

MATTHEW

I stood in shock. The moment happened so fast and suddenly, I didn't know how to react. *Should I scream? Should I run? Should I get help?*

Here's the problem: My little sister decided it would be a brilliant idea to yank on a bunch of boxes labeled "FRAGILE," and what do you know? The boxes started toppling over one by one FROM THE TOP SHELF. They hit the gray tile floor with a thud as loud as a jumping elephant, and all the glass ornaments inside the box spilled out and shattered! Aaliyah is something like four feet tall. How was she even able to move those boxes in the first place?

And the solution? Well, there isn't one. I thought about pretending that I didn't know Aaliyah, but it was no use. It was too late. Everyone raced over.

MIKE HARPER

I heard the sound of shattering glass from inside the building, and all I could think about was how much money this was going to cost me.

Aaliyah

The boxes went tumbling down from the top shelf, hitting the floor with a thud, and shattering all the ornaments. I stood on the ladder, wide-eyed and frozen. Everyone in the entire store came sprinting over.

"Hey! Is that your kid up there?!" an employee shouted at Matthew.

"Do I look like I could be the father of a kid that old?!" Matthew yelled back.

I saw Cami running over, her face flushed and her eyes bulging out of her head. She stopped in her tracks, and then ran back outside. Seconds later, she came back in with Mom and Dad. All the other customers pulled out their phones and took pictures. Every single one of the employees were shouting at me and Matthew. I felt awful. I couldn't imagine how much money Dad was about to end up paying! There was only one thing I could think of to save me from an entire new world of problems.

I did it.

"Mommy! These people are yelling at me! Come save The Baby #1!"

13

The Missing TV

* * *

Meanwhile, back at the house...

Grandma Agnes

Pearl and I both admired that modern-day television our granddaughter got. When the family left, we decided to bring it home with us. We'd put it in my house, and Pearl could visit me every day to learn the controls. We'd give it back when we saw them on Christmas in three weeks, but for now we're going to become trendy citizens.

We called Ricky, our motorcycle trainer, to help uninstall the artifact and load it into our truck. He's a strong young man who's taught us everything we need to know about riding motorcycles. The three of us took the television off the wall, hauled it downstairs, and carefully carried it outside. Ricky loaded the television in the back of our truck.

We got so hot we had to take off our leather motorcycle vests. It was hard work, but we are two tough grannies! We thanked Ricky for his help, and promised we'd bring our new friends, Ethel and Dolores, to him for motorcycle training. We got in the truck to drive back home with the TV wobbling in the back.

MATTHEW

Aaliyah saved herself at the hardware store by telling Mom that she was being yelled at. Dad ended up having to pay $300 for everything Aaliyah broke, but she didn't even get in trouble at all! If I did that, do you have any idea what would happen to me?

"Your family is banned from my store for life!" the manager yelled at us when we left.

"Oh yeah?! It's not like we'd ever come back anyway!" Mom fought back. People kept taking pictures. Dad walked away pretending he was looking at items in another aisle. Cami looked mortified. We left without getting a tree.

Camille

Sometimes I wonder how I am part of this family.

Aaliyah

That was embarrassing. Everyone was staring at me. The manager looked like he had steam coming out of his ears! The worst part was that we never got our tree. Dad said tomorrow he'd leave the house and get a tree from a forest, because of the "banned for life" policy that's been placed on our family at the hardware store. He said there was no way he'd take us to any Christmas tree lot ever again.

Tomorrow will be my first day back at school after Thanksgiving break. When we got back home, I went up to my room to pack my backpack. I immediately realized my TV was missing! I knew Dad had something to do with this! He's been jealous of my TV since day one! I ran downstairs to confront him, but when I got to the living room, I realized it wasn't Dad who stole my TV.

MATTHEW

When we got home, Dad slumped in the living room and turned on the TV as usual. It was the news.

"Breaking news! Two elderly women with a purple dog have caused a serious traffic jam on the highway near downtown Las Vegas! We are getting reports that they

had an ultra-wide television, estimated to be valued at $4,000 in the back of their truck. According to eyewitnesses, the truck hit a rock and the TV 'flew out into the middle of the road.' The TV was then run over, causing damage to another vehicle with several others getting flat tires. Angry drivers are in a stir. Miraculously, there are no reports of injuries. The women are being taken in for questioning now, as police have arrived at the scene to investigate and clean up the shattered television. More will be reported once we obtain new information. In the meantime, avoid the freeway and take side roads instead. Stay tuned for continued coverage on Channel Three News."

Aaliyah

Grandma Pearl and Grandma Agnes were on the news for the second time in less than a week. Wow. And just like that, my TV was gone. I didn't even know what to think.

I woke up the next morning and got the camera from Matthew's balcony while he ate breakfast. I couldn't wait to see the aliens! I didn't have time to watch it just then, though. I shoved the camera in my backpack and got ready to go to school. Time to spend another long day at Cactus City School. Three more weeks until my next break. Let's do this.

14

The New Student

MATTHEW

Today was supposed to be a peaceful, quiet day at home. Aaliyah would be at school, Mom would be out doing who-knows-what, and Dad would be in the woods getting us a Christmas tree. Cami would be here with me, but that doesn't matter because she's never a problem. No grandmas, little sisters and their mischievous friends, parents, or dogs.

"Baby #2 and Baby #3!" Mom came strutting into the room wearing expensive-looking new heels. "I'm going to take The Baby #1 to school, then I'm going to the nail salon, then the hair salon, and then the mall to buy a new outfit to wear when I go shopping tomorrow with my bestie, Barbara. I hired a babysitter to look after you guys. She should be here soon!"

Cami looked up from her book and I looked up from my video game. A babysitter? Aaliyah went into the garage to wait for Mom, who was packing her one thousand lip glosses into her purse.

Turns out, Mom wasn't joking about the babysitter thing! A few seconds later, the doorbell rang, and a girl who looked around thirteen years old, maybe fourteen, was welcomed inside. I watched in complete shock. But part of me wasn't *that* shocked. It *is* Tammy Harper, after all.

"Hey there, you must be Mrs. Harper! I'm Shelby. I'm here to watch your babies for the day." she said to Mom.

Oh, no! I screamed in my head.

"Oh, yes!" Mom screamed in her face. "Come right this way!" Shelby, the "babysitter," came into the living room with Mom.

"Can I take them for a walk in their strollers this morning?" Shelby asked.

"Of course you may! Here's Camille and Matthew!" Mom pointed at us.

"Okay, cool," Shelby said, sounding a little confused. "Now, can you show me where the babies are?" I felt very worried, and I could tell Cami did as well. We were about to be humiliated.

Mom looked like she was going to laugh. "Honey, I just did."

Aaliyah

When I was leaving the house to walk to the bus stop, Mom told me to stay back because she was going to drive me. I thought it was weird since I usually ride the bus. I miss second grade when Matthew would drive us to school together. He'd drop me off at the elementary school, then drive over to his high school. Even with Mindy and all my friends being on the bus, it just wasn't the same.

I asked Mom why she was driving me. Her answer horrified me.

"I hired a babysitter to watch over your big brother and sister for the day. I needed to stay a little longer to let her in, and I don't want you walking to the bus stop alone." A babysitter? My mother is nuts!

When I got to school, there was a new boy in my class named Nico. I decided to befriend him. I invited him to play with me and my friends at recess to make him feel welcome. He seemed like a regular kid at first, but I had no idea what I was in for.

Mindy

I met up with Aaliyah when I got to school. For some reason, she wasn't on the bus this morning. I'm a fourth grader, and she's a third grader, so we couldn't stay together for long. I went to where her class lines up each day before school. There was a new student in her class named Nico. He had just moved to Vegas.

"Let's ask him to play with us at recess," Aaliyah tells me. We're the two most popular, outgoing kids at school. We are friends with pretty much everyone, and we are the ones who run the games at recess. Not in a bossy way, though. We're just leaders and trendsetters. Everyone wants to play with us.

I'm sad that next year, our lunches and recess would be at different times. I'd be with the fifth and sixth graders, and Aaliyah would still be in the third and fourth grade group. What I was most worried about was middle school. When I'd start seventh grade, which didn't seem too far away, I wouldn't even see Aaliyah. We'd be in separate buildings and taking different buses. I once overheard the teachers talking. They were saying how they couldn't wait until I got to middle school. That way they only have to deal with Aaliyah and not both of us.

MATTHEW

Mom walked out the door as if she'd done nothing strange at all. Shelby paced around the living room looking confused.

"Can one of you please explain what's going on? Why do you need me here? And, how come there's an entire bedroom set in this living room?"

Cami closed her book and tried telling Shelby that our mom is just weird and that we weren't like that. "Really, we didn't even know you were coming until you were here," Cami explained.

"Sure..." Shelby still wasn't buying it.

"Shelby, how long are you supposed to stay here?" Cami asked nervously.

"Well, your interesting mom told me until 5:30 tonight." I looked at the clock. 8:22 a.m. Oh man. This is going to be an awkward day.

Tammy Harper

I mean, they said they wanted to be treated like babies... hehehe.

Aaliyah

"Hey Nico, what did you do over Thanksgiving break?" I asked.

"Well, my dad is an astronaut and I went to Jupiter with him. I was also on the news and got famous for being the first person on that planet!"

Everyone stared at him. You can't go to Jupiter! First of all, it would take six years to make it there, and even if you did make it, you couldn't walk on it! Jupiter is entirely made up of gas, so you'd die!

Please. Besides, I was the one who was *actually* on the news.

Camille

Matthew and I tried telling Shelby that we didn't need her and that she could just call someone to get her.

"I took the city bus here. I don't have any other money for a bus ticket, until your mom gets back to pay me for the nine hours I'm supposed to be 'babysitting' you guys. My parents are working, so they can't get me. Believe me, if I had a choice, I'd already be gone." She snickered at us.

"Shouldn't you be in school?" Matthew asked.

"My school doesn't start until Wednesday."

"What grade are you in?"

"Eighth."

I felt terrible. She was only in eighth grade?! I really wanted Shelby to leave, so I offered to give her some of my own money for a bus ticket.

Shelby beamed. "Thank you! Thank you so much!" She took my money and ran out the door as if it were a marathon.

Shelby

Good riddance, weirdos!

15

The Kid at the Football Field

MATTHEW

When Shelby left, I decided to put down my video game and drove over to a nearby field to practice football drills. I wanted a Turbo Ball 2000 football so bad and hoped to get one for Christmas. When I arrived, there was one other guy out there about my age.

"Hey," he said to me.

"Hi," I answered.

"I'm Bryce. Did you know that I am a professional athlete?"

"Really?" I asked. "Wow!"

"Yeah. I'm so good at sports. One time, I swam across the Mediterranean Sea faster than a shark." I gave him a look. *Okay...*

"And one time, I threw a basketball and it went all around the world. Then, it went into outer space and then fell and went right through the hoop, and I scored!"

I just stood there, not knowing what to say. *Should I get away from this kid?* I wondered. Bryce continued lying to me about his "amazing athletic skills." He said he won sixty-two Olympic gold medals, that he went to different countries because he was so good at martial arts, that he hit a tennis ball so hard it landed on a cloud, that he did a backflip holding a bowling ball and got a strike, and much more. The lies were so over-the-top.

"It was nice talking to you, but I have to go." I packed up my things and ran to my car, determined to get away from that guy.

Aaliyah

At lunch, I decided to go to the bathroom with Mindy to watch Matthew's tape and find out if my theory was right about him being an alien.

"Wait! You guys stay here! I have another story to tell!" Oh great. Nico has been telling a bunch of lies this whole day. What did I have to listen to now? I sat down next to my friend Margaret, and Nico began.

"One time when I was stranded in the middle of the ocean, I met a goldfish and it was able to speak English! I still have the goldfish and we're best friends!" Everyone on the table groaned. We were all getting so sick of it! I decided to play along, though.

"Okay, what's its name?"

Nico looked at me, desperately trying to find something to say. He was lying and he knew it. "Ummmm, Margaret! Yeah, Margaret! That's its name!"

Everyone rolled their eyes at each other. Nobody even knew what to say at that point.

"Liar," the real Margaret whispered to me. I nodded my head in agreement.

When I got home after school, I went up to my room to watch the video, but I felt bad because I knew Mindy would really want to watch it with me. So, I decided to save it for later.

"Aaliyah. I had the weirdest day." Matthew came barging into my room without even knocking.

"Actually, I did, too," I replied.

"Mom hired a babysitter for me and Cami. And not just any babysitter! This girl was like, thirteen years old! Then, I went to the football field to practice, and this teenager there started talking to me. It was all lies about him being a professional athlete!" Matthew listed out all the lies, which made me think about my own day.

"No way. A new kid joined my class, and he lied about everything, just like the guy you met at the football field! He said he went to China and fell off a zip line, then was dead for a few days but came back to life! And he apparently has a goldfish named Margaret who he found in the ocean!"

"Who names a goldfish *Margaret*?" Matthew scoffed.

I thought about Dad, who was still out somewhere in a forest looking for a tree. I wondered if he found one yet.

16

Owl on the Loose!

Camille

Mom and Dad got home at around the same time later that evening. Dad was carrying a Christmas tree and a few boxes of ornaments!

"Children?!" Mom yelped. "Where is the young lady who was babysitting today?"

I pulled her aside. "Mom, listen to me. That girl is in eighth grade! Do you know how weird that is? I was SO humiliated! I gave her money for a bus ticket so she left."

"Well, you told me you wanted me to start treating you like The Baby #1, so I did." She started laughing.

"Mom! No! I said I wanted you to stop causing scenes out in public and to be nicer to people! I didn't mean I wanted to be treated like an actual baby!"

"You should see the look on your face, Camille! That's what you get for disrespecting me and my parenting!"

I gritted my teeth. I couldn't stand the behavior of the Original Mom, but the New Mom was even worse. I told her she could just go back to normal and care about only Aaliyah.

"Oh, thank goodness," she sighed. Let's hope she follows through.

Later that night while we ate dinner on the floor—since the table burned down back at Thanksgiving—it sounded like noises were coming from the tree. I shook it off. What would it possibly be anyway?

As I was sleeping on a mattress in Aaliyah's room that night, I heard what sounded like an owl coming from somewhere inside the house. I thought it was bizarre since I never heard owls in our neighborhood before.

"Aaliyah," I whispered. I shook her awake.

"That's my name," she moaned sleepily.

"Listen carefully." And there it was again! It had to be an owl!

"Cami, did you just hear that?" Aaliyah sat up and whispered with her eyes wide open.

"Yes! That's why I woke you up! To see if it was real or if I had just imagined it!"

It sounded like it was coming from downstairs and not outside.

"C'mon! We need to check this out!" I grabbed a flashlight from the closet where Mom and Dad keep linens and household supplies. I headed downstairs, with Aaliyah following close behind. We carefully crept toward the sound in the living room.

Aaliyah

Cami and I knew what we'd heard. It was definitely an owl. We couldn't see one, though. That's when I realized it wasn't any "owl." It was the aliens that Matthew talks to! I ran back upstairs and flung open his bedroom door.

"I KNEW IT!" I shouted, as loud as I possibly could. Wait a second... The room was dark, and Matthew was asleep in his bed. Where were the aliens? I had swung the door open so hard that it hit the wall with a *boom*.

"Aaliyah Jasmine Harper, it is 2:00 a.m.! What in the world are you doing?!" Dad came running down the hallway, with Mom trailing close behind.

"Children! What is going on?" Mom looked like she was having a facial. She was in a bathrobe and her face was covered in a mud mask that smelled like fake strawberries. Before I could answer, Cami started screaming downstairs!

"AAAAH! MOM! DAD! COME QUICK!" Me, Mom, and Matthew ran downstairs, but Dad rolled his eyes and went back to bed.

"Hoooot. Hoooot." It was the noise again! I looked up, and to my horror, there was an owl in the living room!

Camille

Aaliyah bolted upstairs for some reason, but I stayed down. I could hear an owl in the Christmas tree! I spread apart a few of the branches, and the next thing I knew, an owl flew out and started going crazy around the living room! I screamed out for help!

Mom, Matthew, and Aaliyah ran downstairs. As soon as he saw the owl, Matthew sprinted back upstairs to get Dad, who had apparently gone back to bed.

"Nobody move." I said calmly. Dad came down the stairs with Matthew, looking bitter.

"Mike!" Mom hissed. "What if it hurts The Baby? You must trap it and get it out of here at once!"

"We can't trap an owl. I have no idea how to do that. But if you're worried, I'll call animal control." Dad groaned and went to the kitchen to make himself a cup of coffee and call animal control. I slapped my forehead. Animal control? It was the middle of the night! *My family.*

MATTHEW

"Can I keep her as a pet? I named her Sprinkles!" Aaliyah said happily, walking over to the owl and waving hello. The owl seemed to like her. That girl has more friends than a children's cartoon character. Dad was on the phone with animal control. Cami and I noticed dozens of bugs crawling up the wall! So not only did our tree have an owl, but it was also filled with bugs!

"To answer your question, Queen Aaliyah, yes! As long as we find a cage for her, you may keep Sprinkles!" Mom said to Aaliyah.

Dad shot her a look. Most people would think Mom was joking, but Dad has lived with her for twenty-five years. Two and a half decades. He knows Mom well enough to understand that she was being serious when she told Aaliyah she could keep the owl.

"No. Aaliyah, we have to get rid of her. Don't worry, she will go back to her own home to be with her family. You guys, this is my house, too. I don't want an owl living in it. Is that even legal in the first place?" Dad took a sip of his coffee. Aaliyah started to do her annoying fake cry. She was literally crying without any tears coming out, like one of those rich, fancy actors you see on TV. Mom totally believed it was real, though.

"You know what, Mike? You were the one who brought home a tree with an owl living in it. Don't turn it around on The Baby. Just look at her! You've shattered her heart, possibly forever!" Mom scolded him.

The doorbell rang. It was animal control. Dad yawned and opened the door. Meanwhile, the owl watched all the commotion from its perch on the top of the tree.

"Hello, we're here for the owl?" A couple of tired, grumpy-looking men stood at our door holding nets and a cage. They reminded me of Dad.

"Yup." Dad mumbled.

"Once you've captured it, bring it to me. My baby is going to keep it." Mom squealed loudly, an inch from one of the animal control officer's ears.

"I'm sorry, but you can't keep wild owls as pets. They must go back to their habitat. And if there's a baby in the house, please go and get him or her out now. You all have to evacuate," he said to Mom. Aaliyah looked very embarrassed.

"She's standing right in front of you, don't you see? You are so condescending and rude!" Mom snarled.

The men exchanged confused looks. Mom squeezed poor Aaliyah's freckled cheek. Aaliyah looked so mad, I almost laughed.

Aaliyah

Mom totally humiliated me! I could tell Cami, Matthew, and Dad were really embarrassed, too.

From outside, I could hear the animal control guys running around the house, trying to catch the owl. It sounded like a war zone.

"Hey Dad," Matthew said. "There were a bunch of bugs crawling up the wall from the tree. You may want to check your car."

Fearing he'd have to spend more money on an exterminator, Dad ran into the garage through the side door. Sure enough, bugs were crawling all over his car.

"I'm sorry, you guys. Unfortunately, there will be no tree this year." Dad mumbled.

The animal control officers were at our house for another hour. The whole thing took so long, it was beginning to get bright out. I was going to be tired all day.

17

The Lilliana Lie

MATTHEW

Animal control didn't leave until around 4:00 a.m. We stayed up for another hour, though, trying to get rid of the bugs. I was exhausted. We all were. I considered myself lucky because I didn't have anything going on during the day. Dad and Aaliyah, on the other hand, didn't have that luxury. They needed to get back up at 7:00 a.m. to go to school and work. Aaliyah had dark circles under her eyes from being so tired. She looked like a zombie.

Dad called an exterminator in the morning. The exterminator spent an hour spraying the bugs in our house.

They had crawled into our fireplace and into anything that was near the Christmas tree. We removed all the ornaments and lugged the bug-infested tree outside to discard of it.

Aaliyah

School that day was miserable. I was so tired I could hardly concentrate. Nico continued with his lies. He told me he was once in South Africa and then floated on a palm leaf across the ocean to the Americas. During recess, he said he got a new dog named Lilliana.

At lunch, Mindy and I went to the bathroom to watch the tape of Matthew. We were so eager to see the aliens!

I pressed play. We watched until the bell rang. Matthew played video games nearly the entire time. He was either on his bed with his gaming console or getting up and walking out of the room. I felt confused. Where were the aliens? Maybe they just didn't come that day. I'd have to set up the camera again.

That night, when Matthew was in the bathroom brushing his teeth, I put the camera on his balcony again. Surely they would show up at some point!

MATTHEW

I couldn't sleep much that night because it was raining, but not just any rain. There was thunder rumbling and lightning flashing! It was just too loud. I put in earplugs to try and block out the noise, but it didn't work.

Aaliyah

I listened to the sound of thunder. It was booming near my window, but in a way, I found it relaxing. I figured the aliens might not come that night, since their spaceship probably couldn't fly in the rain. Oh well, I guess I'll have to wait another day to record Matthew.

UH OH! I sat up in bed, and my head started to pound with fear. The camcorder! It was out on the balcony in the rain! I lied in my bed the rest of the night concerned I might get in trouble if the camcorder got ruined!

That morning, I ran over to Matthew's balcony, but the camcorder wasn't there! It had probably gotten knocked down by the wind. I went downstairs to the driveway, my hair getting soaked with rainwater. I hoped that maybe someone had retrieved it, but the chances of that were slim. I went back inside and asked everyone if they'd seen it.

"No, Aaliyah, I haven't. You were the one who borrowed it. That was my camcorder, and if you can't find it, you're going to have to work to replace it," Dad told me. I shuddered. I didn't want to have to do any work, so I knew I had to find it.

Later that day at school, I thought it would be funny to keep playing along with Nico's lies. I asked him how his fake dog, Lilliana, was doing.

"Who's Lilliana?" Nico looked at me like he didn't have a clue what I was talking about.

"Your new dog, remember? You said you got her the other day." I thought of every single sad thing that had ever happened to me to stop myself from laughing.

"Ohhhh. Yeah! My new puppy!"

"Yeah. How's she doing? Maybe I could come over to your house sometime to meet her," I said.

"Well actually, you can't meet her. Lilliana died last night in a car accident." Nico looked so guilty! That was the fakest thing I'd ever heard. I had to bite down on my lower lip to hold in my laughter!

"Well, I'm sorry she died," I said and walked away. I hope he'd realized he had been caught in his lie and wouldn't lie anymore.

Delaney

Mindy has been coming home from school with a story about aliens or some weird stuff nearly every single day. She won't tell me why. Last night, Mom came into my room to talk to me.

"Delaney, is it you who's been filling Mindy's head with stories about aliens coming down to Earth? And that schools are science labs used to study teenagers? And that teenagers are actually aliens in disguise?" She stared me down, trying to make me uncomfortable.

I looked at her, confused. "What are you talking about?"

"She's been talking nonstop about it, and she doesn't like to be around you because apparently you're an alien, too." Mom gave me an angry look.

"WHAT?! No! I have no idea what any of that means! Maybe a kid at school told her," I suggested.

"Okay. I'll talk to Mindy some more." Mom left my room. I thought about it. I'm 99% sure this alien thing has something to do with Aaliyah.

18

The Two Invitations

ZOEY EMERSON

My daughter has been talking nonstop about an alien invasion. I'm getting tired of her constantly telling me these stories, and I wanted to find out who has been giving her this information so I could put an end to it.

"Mindy, who is telling you about these aliens? I just talked to Delaney and she said she has nothing to do with this." Mindy looked at me. *Come on*, I thought. It was 10 p.m., and I was tired and wanted to get to bed.

"No, it wasn't Delaney. Aaliyah has been trying to get me to watch videos of Matthew boarding alien spaceships. She's the one who keeps talking about it," Mindy said.

I knew it. That girl is the worst influence on my daughter. And I do not like her parents at all. My husband and I agree that the only reason we still talk to that senseless family is because our girls are friends and because of Matthew and Delaney's relationship.

I want to call Tammy and fill her in on what her daughter is saying, but I know there would be no point in speaking to her about it. She is the type of parent who believes their child could never do any harm in the world. There is no way she'd ever talk to Aaliyah about her behavior. Tammy is the reason Aaliyah is such a problem.

Strange enough, though, the following day around the time Mindy left for school, I got a call from Tammy.

Tammy Harper

Mikey-poo and I have agreed to invite the Emerson family over for Christmas Eve! The children would love to play! I called Zoey to tell her the fantastic news!

"Would your family like to join us for Christmas Eve?"

She said they would love to, but only after she asked who was going to be there. However, she said things about The Baby that were extremely spiteful and loathsome! Ohhhhhhh myyyyyyy!!!!!!!!!!!

Zoey Emerson

Mike and Tammy invited us over for Christmas Eve. I accepted, as it would be good to spend the holidays with someone who has kids. For once I'd like to have a holiday where my girls aren't bugging me. With other kids as a distraction, I figured it might be possible. Plus, Tammy mentioned Grandma Agnes and Grandma Pearl wouldn't be attending. We talked for a bit longer, and I decided to tell Tammy about the things Aaliyah has been saying to Mindy. Maybe since Mike is right there, the conversation would go okay.

"Please talk to Aaliyah, because I don't want Mindy hearing that anymore." I was being as polite as I could, but of course Tammy still had to get offended.

"How dare you insult The Baby like that?! You are no longer invited to our home for Christmas! Over my dead body will you ever come here again!" She screamed through the phone. I rolled my eyes and said nothing.

Mike chimed in. "Tammy, you can't just uninvite someone like that. She already said they were coming. Yes, Zoey, we will talk to Aaliyah." Then they hung up on me.

So... are we going there for Christmas or not?

Aaliyah

When I was getting on the school bus at the end of the day, Nico stopped me. *Lovely. What does he want now?*

"This is for you, Aaliyah." He handed me an envelope. Aaliyah Harper, it read on the front. I wasn't about to listen to another lie, so I boarded the bus as soon as possible. Mindy was waiting for me at our usual seat. She had gotten an envelope, too. We opened them up.

You're invited!

What: Nico Lyington's 9th birthday

When: December 14th, at 4:00 p.m.

Where: 28455 Pale Moon Drive (Nico's house)

We will watch a movie, eat popcorn, and have fun!

Hope to see you there!

Kinda ironic how his last name is "Lyington." Seems like lying runs in the family. At first, Mindy and I agreed that there was no way we'd go. But then I got home and came up with a great idea.

MATTHEW

When Aaliyah got home from school, she asked Mom about attending a birthday party a week from now. As usual, Mom is now going to make me take her. I saw the invitation. It was for that Nico kid who she doesn't even like! How much do you wanna bet that the only reason she wants to go is to annoy me because she knows I would have to take her?

I went up to her room to try and talk her out of it.

Aaliyah

This birthday party would be the perfect opportunity to call Nico out on his lies. I took out a spare sheet of paper and wrote down my plan.

The day of the brthday, rite befor we leve, I wil go owt to owr gardin were Mom has plantid sum flowrz. I wil pik a few roziz and put them in a bowkay. Wen I git to the party, I wil tel Nicos mom, "Oh my goodnis, I am so sory abowt Lilliana," and giv her the flowrz in simputhy. Then she is goin to ask who I was toking abowt. And I wil say, "Your dog..."

!! NICO LYINGTON HEER I COME !!

This was going to be so amazing! I couldn't wait. Maybe it will make him stop lying so much. Matthew came barging into my room, and I told him about my plan. He thought I was a genius, and we totally agreed this would be the best takedown of all time!

19

Surgery Gone Wrong!

Camille

Today we continued decorating our house for Christmas. It was too bad we didn't have a tree, but I kept my hopes high that maybe all the other decorations would be cool. Mom said that she was going to go to the store to buy some new things for decorating.

"Tammy, if you really think we need new decorations, then you can get some, but it has to be *decorations*. Not a TV or a bedroom set or anything crazy," Dad said.

"Don't worry, I'm just getting some new stockings for the children!" Mom skipped across the room, grabbed her purse, took a selfie, and left for the store. I had a bad feeling about this.

Dad brought down the boxes filled with Christmas decorations from the attic. We ran into a problem, of course.

Grandma Agnes and Grandma Pearl's furniture. Our living room was entirely packed with it. Mom had bought that furniture from the same store she bought Aaliyah's TV, so we couldn't return any of it. Dad decided to sell it instead.

We spent the next hour and a half disassembling the furniture and bringing it outside. Dad put up a sign that said: "FURNITURE FOR SALE. PRICE RANGE: $25-$300, DEPENDING ON ITEM."

We finished setting everything up. We sat there in the cold waiting for someone to check out our stand. Cars zipped by without even looking at us.

By the time Mom got home, we still hadn't sold a thing. The only customer we'd had was a woman who picked up a photo frame, examined it, then put it back on the table and walked away. Why does our family always have the worst luck with literally everything?

"Children! Mike! Come see what I bought!" Mom yelled from inside the house. I felt my heart thumping inside my chest. I was nervous to see what she got.

On the table were four stockings. They each had an "A" printed on the front. All four of the "A's" were in a different style.

"Mom, why are there only four? There's *five* people in our family. And why do they all have an "*A*" on them?" Matthew said. He picked up a stocking and made a face.

"Well, I couldn't decide what type of '*A*' The Baby would like best, so I decided to just get all four! After all, she deserves it! I guess that just means Santa will have to bring her extra presents!" Mom giggled and walked away with an exaggerated hip movement. *Jeez. Typical Tammy Harper.*

"I'm sorry you guys," Dad told me and Matthew. "If you want, I'll take you both to the store and buy you whatever stocking you want."

"Nah, Dad, that's okay," Matthew said. "Our fireplace isn't going to fit two more stockings on it. Besides, we still have our old stockings. No need to buy new ones."

We continued to sit outside bundled up in jackets, hoping someone would be willing to stop and check out our stand. Nobody did.

To get people's attention, Mom got a jingle bell and waved it in the air, singing Christmas tunes as loud as she could.

"On the first day of Christmaaaassssss my true love Mikey-poo gave to me, a pair of sparkly diamond earrings! Jingle bells! Jingle bells! Jingle all the waaaayyyyy!" She started making opera noises. Dad looked at her and forced out a smile. People on the sidewalk turned their heads to stare at us, and neighbors poked their heads out of their windows to give us dirty looks. They probably thought we were crazy. Suddenly, I wished we could go back to being ignored.

In the middle of her third song, Mom got a call from Aaliyah's school. They didn't have good news.

Aaliyah

Science lab is always the most fun school activity. I love doing experiments, so I was excited to hear that we'd be going to the lab after recess! Mrs. Smith, my teacher, got the class into a straight line, and we made our way down to the lab.

At the lab, there were boxes filled with fake skeletons and diagrams. Mrs. Smith told us to find a partner. I paired up with Margaret. She was the girl whose name got used in Nico's lie about finding a goldfish in the middle of the ocean.

Last year, since there had been twenty-seven kids in the class, Mrs. Greyson, my teacher back then, made us do groups of three. This year, there are twenty-eight of us. Well, there *were* twenty-eight. But then Nico joined. So now, there was going to have to be a group of three. Nobody wanted Nico in their group. People have gotten sick of his lying. Mrs. Smith saw that he needed a partner, so she made him come to our group since I was his first friend at the school. I was trying to be nice, but Margaret isn't a fan of Nico. And not to be mean or anything, but she isn't the best at school, either. This was going to be hard, dealing with the two of them.

Mrs. Smith came by our table. She gave us a box of fake eyes, ears, kidneys, and hearts. We were supposed to perform a pretend surgery like real doctors. I set up for the experiment and got to work.

I worked for a while and started to get angry with Nico and Margaret. They were doing ABSOLUTELY NOTHING to help! I was the only one who was working! While I was busy trying to get us a good grade, Nico twiddled with his thumbs and Margaret doodled on her notebook. So annoying!

I grabbed a fake eyeball. "Hello, Dr. Aaliyah here! Today I will be performing surgery on this eyeball," I said. Then, I shoved my finger into the small fake eye. Quickly, I realized that I shouldn't have.

I tried to pry my finger from the eyeball.

"Um, Margaret? Nico? I need help!" My finger was STUCK in the fake eyeball. Margaret and Nico were staring off into space and not paying attention. They reminded me of Dad. Asleep with their eyes open. Mrs. Smith came over to help me.

"I think your finger is... embedded in it." Mrs. Smith yanked and pulled, but the eye wouldn't budge.

"Here, let me get a bucket of soapy water. That should loosen it up a bit," Mrs. Smith said nervously. I sat there with my hand in a bucket of soapy water for thirty minutes, and she sent someone to get the nurse. The entire class was huddled over me, trying to investigate, except for the student Mrs. Smith had sent to get the school nurse. The nurse came over and said there was nothing she could do about it. I felt like our nurse never does anything. Like if somebody had a heart attack, she would probably give them a bandage. After the nurse and my teacher tried to pry the eyeball off again without making any progress, Mrs. Smith called 911. I thought it was over-the-top, but they were worried about breaking my finger or peeling my skin off and they didn't want to take any chances. I was humiliated.

"Aaliyah, we called your mom, too. She is on her way over," Mrs. Smith says, concern edging her voice. Now that Mom is getting involved, we both knew it was only going to get worse.

Mindy

I was very bored in class today, so I asked to go to the bathroom. I didn't have to go. I just wanted to leave for a few minutes, get a breath of fresh air, and stretch out my legs. As I walked outside, I saw a firetruck on the blacktop. I was dying to know what was going on, so I got a little closer. I saw someone sitting on a bench surrounded by firefighters, their hand in a bucket of water. It looked like... Aaliyah?!

Camille

"Hello?" Mom answered her phone. A worried look came over her face. And then came the screaming.

"TELL THE BABY I WILL SAVE HER! DO NOT BE AFRAID! I WILL BE THERE IN TEN MINUTES MAXIMUM!" She put on a quick layer of lipstick, then ran to the car, her annoying high heels clicking on the concrete. Dad, Matthew, and I had been standing outside for a long, long time trying to sell all the grandmas' furniture, but we hadn't made a single sale. Why do we always have such terrible luck with everything? Pedestrians stopped to stare at Mom. I wondered what was going on with Aaliyah.

Aaliyah

As if the day hadn't already been going bad enough, Mom showed up while the firemen worked on my hand.

"You could have broken my child's finger! What is the matter with you?! That toy is a hazard. I demand it be disposed of because I never want another parent or child to suffer!" she howled at Mrs. Smith, the principal, and the school nurse. Embarrassed, I closed my eyes and looked down. Don't pity me, though. I've been dealing with this since the second I entered this world, so I've adapted to it by now.

* * *

With the help of a blade, the firemen were eventually able to get that plastic eye off my finger. I was so relieved and couldn't wait to get home. I had no idea I was in for an unpleasant surprise when we got there.

20

Customers

MATTHEW

When Aaliyah got home from school, Mom brought her into the living room to show her all her new stockings. Aaliyah seemed extra happy, since she'd get 4 times more presents from Santa Claus. I went back outside to our furniture sale. Someone pulled over. Two people got out of the car: A boy who looked Aaliyah's age and a woman who I assumed was his mom.

"Hi, we just moved here, and we were thinking about purchasing some furniture for our new home. This is a nice bed," the lady said to Dad.

I guess the boy must've known Aaliyah because he yelled, "Hi Aaliyah! Is this your house?"

Aaliyah's jaw dropped open and a look of dread crossed her face. "Oh, um, hi Nico. What are you doing here?" Wait a second... Nico? That was the kid who told Aaliyah all those lies! I sat down to watch.

"My mom and I were driving home from school and saw the furniture sale. There might be something we can put in our new house." Nico reminded me of Bryce, that kid I met at the football field who lied about being invincible and whatnot. He actually looked exactly like Bryce. A mini twin of him. And, he was a liar, too! I couldn't wait until Nico's birthday party so Aaliyah could call him out on his lies.

"Aaliyah-Bubbiya, why don't you show him your pretty princess room?!" Mom shouted. Aaliyah looked at her. I could tell she was so mad. I tried to hold back a laugh!

"Come on," Aaliyah said flatly and motioned for Nico to come with her.

Aaliyah

I brought Nico up to my room.

"Do you have any cool toys?" he asked.

"Yeah, they're all in that toy box," I pointed.

Nico said he was thirsty and hadn't eaten anything since lunchtime. I was pretty hungry myself, so I went downstairs to get us some snacks and water. When I got back up to my room, I kicked myself for leaving him unattended. It was the most enormous mess I'd ever seen.

"Wow, Aaliyah, you have so many toys!" Nico was on the floor, along with every single thing I owned. It was like the time Chicken got out of his cage and chewed up the hotel room while we were ice skating. (Or, I should say, when everyone was trying to get me out of that bathroom.)

"Nico! What did you do to my room?" I yelled. This was going to take forever to clean! Nico looked confused about why I was raising my voice. What is his problem? Mom and Mrs. Lyington came up to my room.

"Woah! What happened in here?" Mom gasped. She told Nico and Mrs. Lyington that they weren't allowed to leave until my room was immaculate.

We spent the next hour in my room, cleaning the mess. Of course, Nico kept using the excuse of not knowing where anything was supposed to go. So really, it was me cleaning up his mess while he just sat there and watched.

Outside, as they walked back to their car, which was now filled with furniture and had a mattress tied to the roof, I saw Nico grab something from the ground. I didn't think much of it at first, but pretty soon, I'd find out what it really was.

21

Christmas Cactus

MIKE HARPER

My family drives me bonkers. However, I did feel bad that the kiddos wouldn't have a Christmas tree this year. I wasn't going to drive a few hours back to the forest and I wasn't going to take my family to any other Christmas tree lot since the last experience I had with them was a disaster. I asked my wife if it was okay for me to go alone to a Christmas tree lot and get us a tree by myself, but as I expected, she said there was no way she'd let me get a tree without "The Baby" approving of the tree first. Typical.

I thought up ways I could get them some sort of tree without Tammy insisting I bring Aaliyah. Suddenly, I had an idea! I will make this a Christmas like they've never seen before.

I went to a local garden shop and purchased a potted cactus. It was a decent size, not too thin, but not very wide either. It was about four feet tall, just a little shorter than my daughter Aaliyah. It had needles here and there, which I felt would be good to hang our ornaments on.

This cactus would represent the parts of my family. We may be sharp, intimidating, challenging, and tough on the outside. But on the inside we are strong and resilient. Or at least, I am.

Delaney

Mindy and I went to Aaliyah and Matthew's house today. Mindy went straight upstairs to find Aaliyah. I found Matthew and Cami downstairs watching television in the empty looking living room. The grandmas' things were gone, and they hadn't moved their furniture back in from the garage. We sat on colorful beanbags on the floor that Matthew brought down from the loft upstairs. Just then, Mr. Harper walked through the garage door wheeling in a cactus on a cart.

"Say hello to your Christmas tree!" He brought the cactus into the living room.

"Mike," Mrs. Harper looked up from her cell phone and said through her bubblegum-stuffed mouth. "Why is there a cactus in the living room? We baby-proofed the house so The Baby wouldn't hurt herself, remember? This cactus is a hazard! She could get poked!" Mrs. Harper said, smacking her gum.

"Aaliyah isn't going to walk over and touch the needles. Besides, it'll be in the corner." Mr. Harper put the cactus in the corner of the wall.

Mrs. Harper rolled her eyes and continued on her phone.

"Okay. Whatever. If The Baby likes it, fine."

Mindy and Aaliyah came downstairs.

"What's with the cactus?" Aaliyah asked.

"It's our Christmas tree. You can put the ornaments on the needles," Mr. Harper said. Cami, Aaliyah, and Matthew excitedly grabbed a box of ornaments and started to decorate the cactus, hanging the ornaments on the needles.

"Girls, you can help decorate, too," Mr. Harper said to Mindy and me with a welcoming look. We each started hanging up ornaments. Aaliyah put a star at the top. Even though it was a cactus and not a Christmas tree, it still felt very festive.

MATTHEW

The cactus may not have been what I was expecting for our Christmas tree, but at this point I was going to be grateful no matter the tree.

By the time we finished decorating, the cactus looked like a big green cluster of decorations. There were so many ornaments it was hard to focus on just one spot. It had colorful Christmas lights wrapped around it, and a big yellow star twinkled at the top. It truly had become our own unique little tree.

22

Matthew's Secret Plan

Mindy

Mom is making me go to Nico's birthday party today. I don't want to, but I know Aaliyah is going as well, so it won't be entirely bad.

MATTHEW

Today is Nico Lyington's birthday party. I'm taking Aaliyah, and Delaney is taking Mindy. Time to see Nico get called out on his lies. Aaliyah picked some flowers to give to Nico's family in sympathy for the fake dog's death, to make it look like she believes the lie about Lilliana.

We got to the birthday party and Nico's mom answered the door.

"Hi Aaliyah! Thanks for coming!" Mrs. Lyington called Nico to come down.

"Happy birthday, Nico! This is for you!" Aaliyah handed him a wrapped birthday gift. Nico took the gift, and Aaliyah continued with her plan. "I'm sorry to hear about Lilliana, here are some red roses." Aaliyah handed Mrs. Lyington the flowers. It took all of my strength not to laugh!

"Oh, um, who is Lilliana?" she asked, confused. Embarrassed, Nico slowly crept backwards away from us. It was the funniest thing in the whole world!

"Your dog... Nico told me she passed away." Mrs. Lyington slapped her forehead. I had to turn around a little bit to let out a small laugh.

"Oh, um, we don't even have a dog. Nico was probably just messing around. What else has he told you?" She looked embarrassed. Nico probably has always been a liar.

"Well, he did tell me that he went to Jupiter with his dad. I think that's pretty cool!" Aaliyah was smiling ear to ear, and Mrs. Lyington's cheeks turned bright red, as red as the roses she was holding.

"Oh, Nico just likes to exaggerate," she said quickly. Nico was trying to hide his face. *That's what happens when you lie. You eventually get caught.*

We heard a voice coming from upstairs. "Nico?! Have you been lying again?" A man stepped out of a room upstairs. I assumed he was Nico's dad. "We just moved in and already you've made a bad first impression!"

"Sorry," Nico mumbled. We walked into the living room, and my jaw dropped open when I saw who was in there.

Aaliyah

I hope calling Nico out on his lies taught him a lesson! We went into the living room. It was decorated with balloons, party streamers, and birthday gifts. There was a boy in there about Matthew's age who looked like Nico. Matthew seemed very surprised to see him.

"Hey, haven't we met before?" the boy asked Matthew.

"Um, yeah. Your name is Bryce, right?" Matthew asked with a lopsided smile. "I met you at the football field recently." That name, Bryce, sounded familiar. Then I realized: That was the kid at the football field that Matthew told me about! The kid who was telling lies about being a professional athlete! He and Nico must be brothers, and they're both the biggest liars! Their poor parents.

More guests, including Mindy, showed up at Nico's house. The majority of them were from school. Us kids went to Nico's room. I couldn't believe what I saw on his desk!

MATTHEW

No. Way. No wonder Nico looks so much like Bryce, and no wonder he is such a liar! They're brothers!

Other guests arrived. They were like me and Aaliyah. Little kids getting dropped off by their grumpy older siblings. Mindy and Delaney came as well. Bryce took me and some of the older siblings out to the backyard to get some food.

"How old are you?" I asked him.

"Seventeen," he said. Bryce knew a few of the older siblings from school. I found out that he just started at mine, Cami's, and Delaney's old high school. Delaney and the rest of the older siblings took off to go about their day.

"Nice to see you again, but I better get going now," I told Bryce.

"Wait, you can stay here!" He seemed like he desperately wanted me to stay. I didn't want to listen to all those lies, but I realized that maybe he needed someone to hang out with. It would probably be better to tell him to stop with all those stories instead.

"Okay, sure I'll stay here a little longer, but can you please stop telling me all that stuff about being a famous athlete? It isn't funny or anything," I told him. Bryce apologized for all the lies he told, and we decided to throw around a football. Bryce told me how he wanted to fit in but didn't know how. I told him that lying will only make people NOT want to hang out with him.

I was glad I gave Bryce a chance because he was actually very funny and nice. He didn't tell any more lies. Turns out, he wants a Turbo Ball 2000 football, too! We planned to play football together when one of us got one. The party was not as bad as I thought it would be and I made a new friend.

Aaliyah

There, sitting on Nico's desk, was Dad's camcorder! I was almost positive it was the one I lost! The screen was cracked, which had probably happened during the storm when it was left on the balcony. So that must be what he picked up when he left our house after getting the grandmas' furniture!

"Hey Nico, where did you get that camera?" I asked. It *had* to be mine. It looked exactly like it, other than the cracked screen.

"Oh, I actually found this the other day on your street when me and my mom bought that furniture from your house." I knew it! I knew that camera was mine! Well, technically Dad's, but it belongs to the Harpers.

"That's actually my camera. I use it to spy on my brother. You wanna know why?"

MATTHEW

Bryce and I had gone to his room to play video games. We were sitting on the floor when I heard a voice I knew all too well.

"My brother Matthew is an alien. In fact, all teenagers are aliens! Your brother Bryce is, too! I have evidence on this camera!"

Hmmm... so Aaliyah thinks I'm an alien? I remembered her saying something to me about that before, but I hadn't thought anything of it. But after hearing her say it again at the birthday party, I came up with a plan.

When the party was over, I dropped Aaliyah off at home and headed to the local craft supply store. I was going to play Aaliyah's game and give her the scare of her life.

Aaliyah

Nico's party was a lot of fun. Nico didn't tell one lie the entire time. I was hoping that calling him out on it taught him a lesson. He gave me the camcorder back.

When we were getting ready to leave, I pulled Nico aside to talk to him in private. "I had a lot of fun here! I liked the game we were playing with those action figures. I hope I get some for Christmas. Tomorrow, let's play during recess. It's our last day at school before break! But Nico, how come you tell lies? I mean, none of it sounds true."

Nico looked at the floor, embarrassed. "I just wanted to sound cool in front of new people."

"Well, you don't sound cool by making things up that are obviously not real. You're cool the way you are. If people like you only because they think these lies are cool-sounding, and not for who you truly are, then they aren't worth your time."

Nico agreed that he wouldn't lie anymore. I left the party feeling good that I was able to help my new friend. A friend who was kind, funny, and now honest. Even Mindy agreed.

23

"911, What's Your Emergency?"

Mindy

Today is the last day of school before winter break. Tonight, I'll be going over to Aaliyah's house for a sleepover! We're so excited! Now that Aaliyah has her camcorder back, we could watch the videos of Matthew boarding the alien ships! Mommy told me that we'll be going over to Aaliyah's house for Christmas Eve. I must admit, we are worried. We don't want a repeat of Thanksgiving. Grandma Pearl and Grandma Agnes won't be there, though, so we have a chance of a normal

Christmas dinner. Delaney has been telling us that if we're *that* nervous about seeing the Harper family, then why don't we just not go? She has a point, but the thing is, it'll be good to see friends on the most special night of the year. And like I said, we won't be with the biggest troublemakers of all time. That would be the grandmas, who were not invited. We had a good chance of staying on Santa's nice list so we could get presents.

Camille

The second Aaliyah left for school, Matthew locked himself in his room and didn't come out, not even for lunch. He wouldn't let anyone in, either. I was curious to know what he was doing. Probably wrapping Christmas gifts. I saw him bring a box full of tape, construction paper, paint, and other arts and crafts materials.

"Matthew? What are you doing in there?" I knocked on his door.

"I'm working on something! Leave me alone!"

MATTHEW

Aaliyah and Mindy are having a sleepover tonight. Apparently, they think I'm an alien and spy on me because they want to see me board a spaceship or whatever.

So this is my plan: At the arts and crafts store I bought some paint and a bunch of cardboard. I'll make a mask out of the cardboard and paint an alien face on it. Then I'll paint my hands neon green. Whenever Aaliyah has sleepovers, she stays awake THE ENTIRE NIGHT! When it gets really late, I'll go into her room wearing the mask, pretending to be an alien. They'll get so scared! I can't wait for tonight!

Aaliyah

When I saw Nico at school the day after his birthday, he was carrying a little bag.

"This is for you for Christmas!" He handed it to me. I opened the bag. Inside was one of the action figures we played with at his birthday party. I'm glad things with him are better. This holiday will be a good one!

After a fun day at school making gingerbread houses and playing holiday games, Mindy and I got off at the same bus stop and walked back to my house. Matthew was in his room the entire afternoon. Was he up to something?

Mindy and I got into bed later that evening. We were going to stay up all night! Maybe we could see the alien ships come to our house to visit Matthew.

MATTHEW

I spent all day preparing for tonight. I had also bought colored construction paper, some with solid colors and others with little patterns at the arts and crafts store. After finishing my project for tonight's BBLS takedown, I made

Aaliyah paper dolls for a Christmas gift to help pass the time. I was so eager to start!

* * *

I looked at the clock. 12:00 a.m. It was midnight exactly. Time to start my plan! The paint on my hands had dried and my alien mask was ready to go.

I grabbed a flashlight and tiptoed over to Aaliyah's room. Mindy and Aaliyah were giggling inside. One of these days, when they are fifteen or older, they'll regret not wanting to sleep when they were younger.

I cracked Aaliyah's door open a bit. How are they still awake? I just don't get it!

I poked my green hand in and shined the flashlight on it. Mindy and Aaliyah went completely silent. I heard a gasp.

"The aliens have arrived!" whisper-screamed Aaliyah. Then, I opened the door a little more and peered through with the green, oval, big-eyed mask I had worked on all day.

After they got a good look, I stepped back and closed the door. I rushed back to my room so I could burst out laughing into my pillow. I was hoping to go to sleep, but the girls had a different idea.

Mindy

The sleepover went downhill fast. Aaliyah and I heard her bedroom door creak open. At first we ignored it, thinking it was the wind, but when a green hand slid inside followed by a huge green alien head, we knew there was something more.

Aaliyah

White light shined through my door. Mindy and I FREAKED. OUT.

"I- It- It- It's- It's the- It's the aliens!" I stuttered, in complete shock. Mindy was covered in cold sweat. She opened her mouth to scream, but I immediately covered it with my hands. We couldn't make one peep! The alien would get us!

"It's Matthew! He really is an alien! Those are his pajamas!" I whispered, terrified! We got up and ran to my closet to hide! The alien, well, Matthew, was standing in my doorway! As soon as the door closed, we caught our breath and buried ourselves under the covers.

"Okay. Here's the plan. We're going to cover ourselves in as many blankets as possible and stay low, then crawl all the way down to the kitchen where the phone is. We need to call 911," I whispered, panting.

Mindy

Aaliyah and I covered ourselves in blankets and crawled downstairs to the kitchen, bumping into walls and furniture along the way. We needed to be quiet, because

Cami was sleeping on the living room couch, which had been moved back now that the grandmas' furniture was gone. She was sleeping there so I could stay in Aaliyah's room.

Aaliyah reached up and grabbed the kitchen phone, dialing 911. I told Aaliyah not to tell 911 that Matthew was an alien because they wouldn't believe us. Grown-ups never believe anything kids say.

"911, what's your emergency?" said the lady on the other end of the line.

"There's something wrong with my brother! He's like... changing colors! He doesn't look like himself!" Aaliyah breathed into the phone.

"Is he turning blue?" she asked.

"No... he's green!" Aaliyah whispered.

"Do you know if he's breathing?"

"I don't know! But he's green!"

"Okay, well when a person changes colors, that usually means they are not breathing. What is your address? I'll send an ambulance."

MATTHEW

I kept laughing to myself and couldn't believe how freaked out Aaliyah and Mindy were! I closed my eyes ready for sleep to take over. About four minutes later, I could hear the sound of sirens. I ignored it at first; they could be going anywhere. But they continued to get louder and louder by the second, all the way up until they reached our driveway. *Oh boy.*

Delaney

Ringggg. Ringggg. I woke up from a good dream about swimming in a river of tasty chocolate milk to the sound of my phone ringing. I checked the clock. What in the world... 12:09 a.m.! Who was calling me this late?! I looked at my phone. It was Matthew.

"Hello?" I asked, annoyed to be rudely awakened.

"D-D-D-D-Delaney, I just messed up really bad," Matthew whispered into the phone.

"What happened?" I said flatly.

"So the other day at, um, Nico's party, I overheard the kids talking. Aaliyah and Mindy were telling all those kids that they think I'm an alien! I decided to mess around with them and sneak into Aaliyah's room tonight wearing an alien mask! I thought they'd get scared for a moment and then forget about it, but what do you know? They called 911! There is a fire truck and an ambulance right below my window!"

I was shocked into silence. Mindy and Aaliyah getting into this kind of trouble didn't surprise me, but Matthew?

MATTHEW

I didn't know what to do. I watched out my bedroom window as paramedics and firefighters hauled a stretcher, oxygen tank, and a ton of medical equipment to our front door! I spoke to Delaney over the phone, panicking.

"Well Matthew, it's Aaliyah and Mindy. What were you expecting? Of course they aren't going to let a prank like that slide so easily," she said, and she was very right. What was I thinking?! If I wanted to play a prank, I should've done it on Cami or someone else. Anyone but them! They are the biggest troublemakers in the universe, no doubt about it!

Aaliyah

We could hear the ambulance arriving. Cami lifted her head from the couch, her hair all messed up from sleeping.

"Huh?" she moaned.

"Don't. Move." Mindy whispered in my ear. "The alien spaceship might still be here!"

Mike Harper

Tammy and I woke up to the sound of sirens. We looked out the window and saw the fire department. If Camille was the one who called, then I'm worried. If Matthew was the one who called, then I'm worried. If it was a neighbor, I might be a little bit worried depending on which neighbor it was. We have some highly annoying neighbors. If it was Aaliyah and what's-her-name, I'm going back to bed.

Tammy Harper

I raced down the stairs at top speed! Ohhhhh myyyyy! What if The Baby was hurt?! I looked up the staircase and saw Mike slumping his way down the stairs, groaning with each step he took.

"Hurry up, Mike! The Baby could possibly be in danger!" I shouted at him.

Mindy

There was pounding and thudding on the front door. The doorbell rang a thousand times. I peeked through the fluffy purple and white striped blanket that Aaliyah and I were hiding under. Mrs. Harper opened the door gracefully while yanking hot-pink foam curlers out of her hair. A group of paramedics holding a medical kit and one of those bed things with wheels (I later learned it's called a gurney) came running in through the door. Mr. Harper was nowhere to be seen.

"Aaliyah, let's make a run for it in three, two, ONE!" We grabbed the blanket and raced to the door screaming.

MATTHEW

Things were getting so out of hand. Mindy and Aaliyah were yelling from downstairs.

"Matthew is an alien! My brother is an actual alien! He's changing colors and looks all green!"

I was truly panicking at that point. I knew Mom and Dad would be furious with me if they found out what I'd done. I grabbed my gigantic homemade alien mask, opened my balcony door, and chucked the mask down to get rid of the evidence, hoping all my problems would be solved. But instead, I made everything a hundred times worse. My alien mask HIT ONE OF THE PARAMEDICS ON THE HEAD!!!!

Aaliyah

"My brother is an alien!" I yelled at the paramedics.

Mom grabbed me. "Queen Aaliyah! Are you hurt?!" I shook loose from her grip. Dad was still trudging down the stairs. When he heard me speak, he slapped his forehead and started going back up.

"Kid, there's no such thing as aliens," said a paramedic. Then, another paramedic came through our door, holding up a big green alien mask.

MATTHEW

In my life, nothing ever goes right. Paramedics were running through the house, asking where the brother who was changing colors was. I listened to them from the crack of my door.

"We don't know! He probably already boarded his spaceship!" Aaliyah and Mindy kept on yelling things about aliens at the firefighters and paramedics.

I only had two options. Either I could go downstairs and confess to everything, or I could pretend to be sleeping. Here's the thing: If I pretended to be asleep, maybe everyone would think that Aaliyah and Mindy were just making things up about seeing an alien, but they would still have the mask as proof so I was sure everyone would still know it was me. If I confessed, there was a high chance I would pass out from embarrassment. But since there are paramedics already here, they'll be able to revive me, right?

I came up with a better idea. I was going to go downstairs and ask what was going on. I figured that if I acted like I had no idea what was happening, people wouldn't think it was me.

Mike Harper

I'm going back to bed and letting Tammy deal with this.

Camille

I hid under the sheets on the couch. Not because I feared being seen by the "aliens," like Aaliyah and Mindy were, but because I didn't want to be seen by the firefighters and paramedics. I wanted to remain anonymous in this very outrageous situation.

TRENT ANDERSON, PARAMEDIC AND PRE-MED STUDENT

First, our department sent our crew in the middle of the night to a house in which a boy might not be breathing. Second, we arrived at the house and heard a couple of little girls screaming something about aliens. Third, a humongous hand-crafted alien mask fell from the sky and bonked me on the top of my head. Fourth, when I stepped into the house, there was a woman calling one of the little girls "Queen Aaliyah," and a sleepwalking man who was probably her husband. Fifth, a boy who looked a few years younger than me came running down the stairs yelling, "I don't know what happened! I swear! I'm innocent!"

I peered into the darkness of the living room. Was that a... cactus... covered in Christmas ornaments? Um... what? *This just keeps getting better and better,* I thought. And then, I saw what looked like a body covered up with white sheets on the couch! It wasn't even moving at all! Oh... my... I walked over to the possibly dead body, my forehead sweating and hands trembling. It might be time to call the police.

I braced myself and yanked back the sheet, revealing a woman who looked around my age. She opened her eyes. They were the prettiest eyes I'd ever seen.

Camille

When I was little, I heard stories about love at first sight. I never understood it until the day my irksome little sister and her best friend called 911 for no reason.

Delaney

Matthew had been too busy panicking to hang up the phone. I didn't want to hang up on him, though, because things were getting juicy. I sat on my bed listening to all the commotion going on. I really hope my parents don't hear about this because if they do, they'd make me dump Matthew for sure.

MATTHEW

I ran downstairs and tried to act confused.

"I really am innocent!" I said. Cami came into the room with one of the paramedics. He was holding my cardboard alien mask. Oh no.

"Wait," Aaliyah looked at me with a worried face. "Matthew, is that green paint on your hands?"

Mindy

Aaliyah and I couldn't believe our eyes. Matthew had painted his hands green, and that alien mask was a piece of painted cardboard! Mrs. Harper went back upstairs, probably to put some lipstick on. I thought I saw Mr. Harper's head peeking out from behind a wall at the top of the stairs, trying not to be seen and looking furious.

"Was this the alien you saw?" one of the paramedics standing with Cami asked me and Aaliyah.

"Wait a minute, Matthew, were you trying to prank us?" Aaliyah was staring at his green painted hands, shocked.

"Um, um, I don't know what you're talking about," Matthew said. The house fell silent.

"You guys, if there is no emergency, then why did you call us? This is not a laughing matter," said a firefighter.

"But we're *not* joking!" Aaliyah turned to the firefighter, truthfulness in her eyes. "There was actually something wrong with my brother. He *was* green! He *did* look like an alien! An alien wearing my brother's pajamas came into my room while me and my friend were trying to go to sleep! Right, Mindy?" She nudged my arm.

"Yes, everything Aaliyah is saying is true," I explained to the firefighter. "We called because we were worried that the aliens would hurt us and were hurting her brother. We thought maybe her brother could be sick. We weren't sure what was happening or what we should do, so that's why we called. I mean, you guys seem to know how to do everything."

I heard the sound of Delaney's voice hissing from Matthew's phone. *"Mindy?! Is that you?! What is going on?! You guys are all crazy!"*

Matthew hung up on her. He looked down at the floor and began to speak. "Well... so... I heard Aaliyah and Mindy talking about how they thought me and all teenagers were aliens, and I just wanted to play a joke on them. It was supposed to be funny. I *intended* to make it funny. I had no idea it would get this bad. I am so sorry for causing you all this trouble, it won't happen again," Matthew told the firefighters and paramedics. He looked like he felt really bad. Mrs. Harper came back out of her room with fifty pounds of makeup on.

A paramedic came over to me and Aaliyah. "I have a little sister, too. When we were kids, I used to do this kind of thing to her all the time. But girls, there is no such thing as aliens," he explained. "I think it was good that you were worried about him, but next time you think someone might be in danger, you need to go and tell your parents or a grown-up right away, instead of trying to handle it by yourself. Understood?"

"Understood," we said at the same time.

"Aliens. Jeez. It's all the video games children play nowadays," I heard one firefighter whisper to another. Why do grown-ups blame everything kids do on video games? I'd die without video games!

Matthew apologized once more, and the firefighters and paramedics packed up their equipment and left. Now THAT is what I call a BBLS adventure!

Camille

What. A. Night. I ended up getting into a conversation with the paramedic who had found me hiding under the sheets from embarrassment. His name is Trent. Trent Anderson. He is my age, pre-med, and is working as a paramedic for experience. I had thought his name sounded familiar, and it turned out we had gone to the same middle school. Supposedly, I looked like a dead person lying on the couch under the sheets like that. We exchanged phone numbers to hang out together while I was in town.

Aaliyah, Mindy, and Matthew all felt very bad. Now don't get me wrong, I was displeased that I had gotten woken up in the middle of the night due to a false emergency, but one good thing did come out of it. Trent.

Mike Harper

Well that was twenty minutes of sleep I missed out on and will never get back.

24

A Harper-Emerson Christmas

Delaney

Today is Christmas Eve. We've been invited to the Harpers' house for dinner. At first, we weren't sure about going because of, you know, the entire Thanksgiving situation. But Mrs. Harper had mentioned that Grandma Pearl and Grandma Agnes weren't coming, so we decided it was okay. It would be more fun to spend Christmas with friends, and in mine and Matthew's case, a loved one.

MATTHEW

I felt absolutely terrible after the alien incident. It was probably the worst I'd ever felt. It was worse than when Aaliyah knocked over all the Christmas ornaments at the hardware store. It was worse than when Mom threatened the hotel manager that she would shut their business down when we were on vacation. It was even worse than when Mom hired the 8th grade babysitter for me and Cami.

Christmas is tomorrow. Mom and Dad decided that they didn't want the grandmas coming over, so they never invited them. After Thanksgiving and Aaliyah's birthday, they left a bad taste in our mouths. We would be having the Emersons over, though. The other day, Dad bought a new table to replace the burned one. We set up red and green plates, Santa napkins, and utensils. The table looked very festive.

I went up to my room and finished wrapping everyone's presents. I gently put the paper dolls I had made for Aaliyah in a gift bag, being careful not to rip them. Honestly, though, Aaliyah is going to destroy those things the second she starts to play with them. All her dolls have chopped off hair and broken necks. I put the bag under our Christmas cactus, excited to see Aaliyah's reaction when she opens my handcrafted present.

Grandma Agnes

Pearl and I received a phone call from my son, Mike, and his very loud wife, Tammy. Since we are no longer invited to any of their parties, they called to check in with us. Probably to make sure we weren't on the road to their house. *Tsk Tsk.* We already had plans anyway. We needed to make up for destroying our granddaughter's modern-day television. We wanted to get her a new one. We just have one problem: Pearl and I don't know where to purchase a modern-day television.

Later that day, we went to visit our pals Ethel and Dolores at the nursing home where they live. They both moved there a few years ago, which is how they met and became best friends. Ethel's olden-day television in her room gave Pearl and me a great new idea.

Aaliyah

Matthew has been wanting a Turbo Ball 2000 football for a long time. Christmas is tomorrow, and I still haven't gotten him a present, so I asked Mom to take me to the sporting goods store a few blocks away to get him the football.

Mom and I left the house, and I even brought my piggy bank with me, so I could buy it for him with my own money.

At the store, I also purchased gifts for everyone else. I bought Mom a hairbrush, Cami a book, and Dad a box of chocolates to eat while he watched TV.

When we got home, I wrapped all the gifts and put them under the Christmas cactus.

The Emersons arrived that evening. Mindy and I went up to my room to play. Dad told us not to get into any mischief.

"Girls don't get into any trouble. Santa Claus is still watching, and if you do anything naughty, he'll skip our houses and you won't get any presents!" He looked like he was so desperately trying to have a peaceful night with no mischief.

Grandma Pearl

Agnes and I needed to replace Aaliyah's television. There were a few olden-day televisions in Dolores and Ethel's nursing home. It reminded Agnes and me of the good ol' days when we were young, back in the 1900s. Since there were extras, Ethel and Dolores generously let us take one to give to Aaliyah.

Me, Agnes, Ethel, Dolores, and Chicken got in the truck and drove to the Harpers' house. We rang the doorbell. That younger girl who is Matthew's girlfriend answered, with the rest of our family standing behind her.

"And so we meet once again, young missy," Agnes said to the girl.

Camille

Trent and I texted each other "Merry Christmas." We've been keeping in touch lately. Matthew and Aaliyah still feel bad about the alien thing, but I wasn't mad anymore. Especially since it led to me meeting Trent.

Tonight at our Christmas Eve dinner, things started out normal. Nobody was being troublesome. Aaliyah and Mindy were trying so hard to be good because they didn't want Santa to fly right over their houses and not give them any presents.

The doorbell rang as we were eating our dinner of ham, cranberry sauce, buttery biscuits, and mashed potatoes that Mom had made. Matthew and Delaney got up to see who was there, thinking it may be Christmas carolers singing outside. But then, we heard barking. A familiar bark. Oh... no! Delaney opened the door and Matthew shouted for us to come over. We couldn't believe who we saw!

Standing outside was Grandma Pearl, Grandma Agnes, Chicken, and two other older ladies. Grandma Pearl was carrying one of those old-fashioned television sets from the 70s or 80s. It was small and had buttons on the front and an antenna poking out of the top.

"Oh, um, what a pleasant surprise! Merry Christmas! Mom, Pearl, who are your friends?" Dad asked.

"This is Ethel and Dolores. We met them at the jail last month when your daughter locked herself in the bathroom, and we got arrested for driving that fire truck," said Grandma Agnes, smiling proudly.

Delaney's face lit up. "Wait, I remember seeing you two with Grandma Pearl and Grandma Agnes back at the hotel! My name is Delaney Emerson by the way. Merry Christmas," she said, shaking their hands.

Mom pulled Dad away from the door. I crept close to hear their conversation.

"I don't know. Should we let them in? I don't want a repeat of Thanksgiving," Mom whispered to Dad.

"Of course, Tammy. I mean, it's Christmas. We can't just turn them away," Dad said. We welcomed the grandmas and their friends inside.

"We brought you presents," Grandma Agnes said. We added extra plates at the table for our new guests and sat down to finish dinner.

Thankfully, the grandmas were on their best behavior and there were no disastrous events during dinner. We all held our breath, unsure of what to expect. Even the Emersons seemed to go along with the new change in plans.

After everyone was done eating, we sat around the Christmas cactus to open gifts.

"Why is your Christmas tree a cactus?" Dolores asked.

"It's a long story," said Matthew.

One of our family traditions is to open one small present on Christmas Eve. Of course, Mom declared that Aaliyah would open her present first.

"Queen of all space and time, which present would you like to open?" she asked Aaliyah.

Aaliyah

I looked over the presents under the Christmas cactus, trying to decide what to open.

"What do *you* guys think I should open?" I asked everyone.

"Actually, Aaliyah, we'd like you to have this. It's to replace that modern-day television of yours that all those rude drivers ran over," Grandma Pearl told me, pointing at the weird TV that looked a hundred years old.

"It's from Ethel and Dolores's nursing home. This TV was worth a lot back in our day," Grandma Agnes said. Kinda odd how it didn't have a remote. *It probably is worth a lot now, too, since it's basically an antique.* I thanked the grandmas and their friends, Ethel and Dolores, for the TV. Even though it wasn't a humongous, shiny, expensive TV like the one I had before, I was still happy to have a TV.

Matthew opened his present next. He chose Delaney's.

MATTHEW

I opened Delaney's present. No... way... IT WAS A TURBO BALL 2000! I was so excited! I couldn't wait to go to the field and practice with it!

Aaliyah opened her mouth wide. She looked very shocked.

"Is there something wrong, Aaliyah?" Delaney asked her.

"I got Matthew a Turbo Ball 2000! Why did Delaney have to?" Aaliyah looked angry. "I bought it for him with my own money!"

Dad turned to her. "It's okay, we can return it. If you want, I can take you to buy him something else when the stores open after Christmas," he told her.

"Matthew, is there anyone else you know who might like that ball?" Aaliyah asked me. "You can give it to them." I was surprised at how generous she was being. It was probably because she knew Santa was watching and she wanted her presents delivered.

I thought about it. "Actually, I *do* have a friend who would. My new friend, Bryce."

Christmas Day

* * *

Aaliyah

Waiting for Christmas always feels like forever throughout the year. But today, when I woke up, it was finally Christmas morning!

I prowled downstairs to the living room and saw a mountain of presents under the Christmas cactus, and candy and small toys in all four of my stockings! I raced back upstairs, bashed through Mom and Dad's bedroom door, and jumped onto their bed, yelling and making as much noise as possible! I ripped off Mom's eye mask. Once they woke up, I flew down the hallway to Matthew's room. His turn!

"Santa's been here, Matthew! Santa's been here!" I pounded on his mattress, then zoomed back to my room to wake up Cami, who was sleeping on the mattress on the floor.

Finally, everyone got out of bed and slowly made their way to the living room, one itty-bitty step at a time. Why do old people take a million years to get up in the morning? It's Christmas for crying out loud!

After what felt like an eternity later, the whole family was seated around the Christmas cactus and we began opening gifts. For some strange reason, I felt just as good watching everyone else open the presents I gave them as I did opening my own.

Later that day, we got a call from the grandmas... and they had news.

25

Mission Accomplished

Grandma Agnes

When we left Mike and Tammy's house on Christmas Eve, Ethel and Dolores invited Pearl and me to start living in the nursing home with them and all their other friends. They informed us of the fun activities we'd get to do there such as watch the olden days channels, play bingo, and knit scarves for our grandchildren. Pearl and I agreed that this would be a good decision. We made arrangements with the people who worked at the nursing home and started packing our belongings. A few weeks from now we will begin our new lives in the nursing home. I'm looking forward to spicing things up at that place with my partners in crime—Ethel, Dolores, Chicken, all the new friends I was going to make at the nursing home, and, of course, Pearl!

A Few Weeks Later

* * *

MATTHEW

A lot had happened over my holiday break. Wild grandmothers, a fire at our Thanksgiving dinner, noisy car rides, a disastrous stay at a hotel, getting banned from a store, an animal and bug-infested Christmas tree, a thirteen-year-old babysitter, and so much more. But I wouldn't say my break had been entirely bad, though. I had a fairly good Christmas, got a Turbo Ball 2000, hung out with my family and friends, and even made a new friend, Bryce. My *crazy* sister and her friend called 911 over my harmless prank, and my *normal* sister ended up getting a boyfriend. I sure hope Mindy and Aaliyah's heads aren't filled with those alien thoughts anymore. I don't think they realize that one of these days, they'll be teenagers, too.

I heard my grandmas are going to be moving into a nursing home with their new friends, Ethel and Dolores. Their neighbors are sure going to be thrilled to hear that news. But that nursing home, on the other hand... it's going to come crashing down!

Today I am going back to college and Cami is going to continue working on her teaching credential. She told me that soon she'll be a student teacher in a real classroom and help the teacher out, so that she has practice for when she becomes a teacher herself. Maybe someday she'll be able to teach at Aaliyah, Nico, and Mindy's elementary school, which also used to be mine, hers, and Delaney's.

Speaking of Delaney, she and her family arrived at our house to say our goodbyes. Delaney and I go to the same university and live in dorms near each other, so we are going to be driving back together. This reminded me of a few months ago when we left for college the first time; meeting at my house, saying goodbye to our families, and leaving together.

The Emersons came inside and we sat around the Christmas cactus one last time. All four of Aaliyah's stockings were hanging on the chimney. We hadn't bothered to take the decorations down yet. I honestly didn't even want to. It was funny, and it symbolized one of the craziest but most fun and exciting holiday breaks of my life!

Delaney

Well, another year down. Matthew and I are leaving now. It's always hard saying goodbye, but I know that goodbyes aren't forever and I'll see everyone again soon. Mindy may get on my nerves, but I must admit... life without her would be dull and boring!

Camille

Winter break is coming to an end and we are all going back to school. I'm looking forward to being able to teach in a classroom. Pretty soon I'll be working as a student teacher to get practice for when I have my own classroom. Matthew and I were thinking maybe I could work at our old school, which is now Aaliyah's school! Who knows? I might...

Mindy

Every night since Delaney left for college, I've called her to talk. I plan on doing that all the way up until college ends. I call it the *Delaney Commitment*. I stick to it every day.

And so that night before I went to bed, I picked up the phone and waited to hear her voice.

MIKE HARPER

My family makes my blood boil, but I must admit, I wouldn't trade them in for all the quiet days or TVs in the world.

Aaliyah

Everyone got together at the end of our holiday break. The last time Matthew and Delaney had to leave was not easy. It seemed as if they'd never return! I was also suspicious about this whole "college" thing because I thought *for sure* that it was a place for aliens! But now I know they are going to college to get an education, not for some make-believe alien experiment.

I said goodbye to Matthew and Delaney. *They'll be back soon,* I told myself. I guess I found out the truth about my brother and all the teenagers in the world. Matthew is not an alien. He's the best big brother ever! *Mission accomplished.*

Five Months Later

* * *

MATTHEW

I got a call from Mom and Dad. A new family is moving into the house next door to ours, right on the day I come back home for the summer. They supposedly have a kid Aaliyah's age... Oh boy, should I be worried?????

To Be Continued...

Author's Note

Dear Friends,

It's been an exciting but challenging adventure with the Harper family and their friends. I even had to take a break during the writing of this book because Tammy and Aaliyah became too much to handle!

I'd like to give a special thanks to the following people for helping BBLS become what it is today: Tracy Atkins, for being my go-to person for everything book related from the very beginning of my author journey. Tanja Prokop, for her award-winning expertise in book design. Tereza Vrkić Šarčević, for her continuous hard work in making my chapter illustrations how I envision them. My cover illustrator and talented artist, David Harrington, for taking what was in my head for the book cover and making my characters real after speaking with me about their personalities. My editor, Rachael Stein, for believing in me, making this book the best it can be, and giving a teen author a chance to grow and learn as a writer. My web designer, Matthew Young, for creating a fun, detailed, and engaging website.

I'd also like to thank all the kids and adults who have read and enjoyed my books and supported me every step of the way. My goal is to make you laugh and I hope I succeeded!

Finally, to my family. Mason, BBLS is all your fault, but in the best way possible. Teta, Jiddo, Gramma, and

Grampa—I love you so much. Thank you for giving me the best parents ever (who are nothing like Tammy and Mike.) Last, my parents. There's a lot of things I want to say, but you already know.

Are people actually going to read this?

Love,
Elena

About the Author

Photo Credit: Pamela Marches Photography

Bestselling teen author **Elena Southworth** was born on July 1, 2007. Elena first knew she wanted to be a writer when she was five years old and had just read her first book by herself. A fan of make-believe stories, she penned some of her own and she was hooked.

Elena hopes her stories become a place where readers can escape and find some great humor along the way. She'd like to be an inspiration as a young author to encourage other children to write books as she has and that nothing is impossible.

Elena's writing has enabled her to contribute charitably by donating dozens of her BBLS books to Children's Hospital of Orange County at Mission Hospital, and Orangewood Children's Home, along with having her book in many classrooms and school libraries. Elena has been invited as a "Meet the Author" guest at several school assemblies to share her love of writing and inspire young authors.

When she isn't writing, Elena enjoys playing piano and video games. She lives in Orange County, California with her mom, dad, little brother Mason, and their puppy, Bo.

The Harpers' Holiday Horror is the second book in Elena's ***Big Brother, Little Sister*** three-book series. Stay tuned for BBLS Book #3, coming soon.

Contact Information:
www.ElenaSouthworth.com
Instagram: @prodigykidspress

Made in the USA
Middletown, DE
14 October 2021